CONTENTS

Author's Note   vii

Story Description   ix

1. Kerrigan   1
2. Dmitry   6
3. Kerrigan   10
4. Dmitry   14
5. Kerrigan   18
6. Dmitry   22
7. Kerrigan   26
8. Dmitry   31
9. Kerrigan   35
10. Kerrigan   39
11. Dmitry   43
12. Kerrigan   47
13. Kerrigan   51
14. Dmitry   55
15. Kerrigan   59
16. Dmitry   63
17. Kerrigan   67
18. Dmitry   71
19. Kerrigan   75
20. Dmitry   80
21. Kerrigan   84
22. Dmitry   88
23. Kerrigan   92
24. Dmitry   96
25. Kerrigan   100
26. Dmitry   104

NEXT BOOK IN THIS SERIES...   111

Other books from Candace Ayers...   113

HERO BEAR

P.O.L.A.R.

CANDACE AYERS

LOVESTRUCK ROMANCE

AUTHOR'S NOTE

P.O.L.A.R. (Private Ops: League Arctic Rescue) is a specialized, private operations task force—a maritime unit of polar bear shifters. Part of a world-wide, clandestine army comprised of the best of the best shifters, P.O.L.A.R.'s home base is Siberia...until the team pisses somebody off and gets re-assigned to Sunkissed Key, Florida and these arctic shifters suddenly find themselves surrounded by sun, sand, flip-flops and palm trees.

Substandard job performance,
Indebted to a sleazy loan shark,
Crushing on a shifter who's out of her league,

Kerrigan is in a heck of a pickle.

Dmitry's not gentle.
He's not the nurturing type.
He's a cold-blooded killer—a P.O.L.A.R. assassin

But, when he steps in to protect her, Kerrigan doesn't see a killer, she sees a
Hero Bear.

KERRIGAN

*I*f I'd ever needed an intervention, it would have been at the moment I decided that moving into the house with all six of the guys from P.O.L.A.R. would be better than living out of my car. I'd chosen to live under the same roof with the guys I spent all day working for. There was such a thing as too much togetherness.

When Serge, the Alpha of the team, found out I'd been living out of my Honda, he made a big stink about it. And, since Roman had recently moved out to live with his new mate, Megan, there was a room vacant. That meant either I stand up to Serge and say no, or I go along with his wishes. I was terrible when it came to confrontation. Especially with an Alpha. So, I guess it wasn't totally my choice to move in. I just didn't decline the request. Still, an intervention would've been nice.

The large, two story bungalow that housed P.O.L.A.R. was prime beach front real estate. Located on the west side of Sunkissed Key, only a short walk from the P.O.L.A.R. office, it was a beautiful, old house on a beautiful white, sandy beach. Rumor was, it had been an old bed and breakfast at one time and, with a little renovating, had been transformed into the house for the team. It was certainly large enough to fit a whole gang comfortably. At least, it should've been. If the guys were normal sized men. They weren't. They were shifters, and the shifters of P.O.L.A.R. made the hallways feel narrow, and the kitchen and dining room laughably miniscule.

Roman had moved out just the day before and I was lugging in the two bags containing all my worldly possessions. I struggled with the garbage bags while Serge and Konstantin watched me. When I paused to take a breath, they both offered to help. I didn't want their help, though. It was embarrassing, especially since I sucked at my job. I could at least carry in my own bag and prove that I actually could do something without screwing it up.

Alexei stepped out of the bathroom and into the middle of the hall grinning at me and shaking his head before disappearing back into his room. I appreciated his hands off approach as I continued to drag the bags up the stairs toward the corridor.

I'd already gotten the suckers up two flights of stairs. The heaviest bag held a collection of books hidden in a blanket at the bottom. I was almost to the door of my new bedroom. Unfortunately, like most things in my life, the move didn't go as planned. The bag advertised as a "heavy-duty steel-sack" tore like tissue paper. The force I'd been applying to pull the weighty bag up the stairs set me off like a rocket and I went flying backwards until I landed on the hardwood floor with a *thud*.

Flat on my back, I stared at the ceiling and groaned. Heavy-duty my ass! Actually, most of the impact had been absorbed by my ass and it stung. Not nearly as much as my ego, though. I couldn't seem to catch a break.

"Damn. You okay?" Serge's face appeared staring down at me wearing what he tried to present as a concerned expression. But I could see him struggling to keep the corners of his mouth down. He was laughing inside.

I gritted my teeth and nodded. "Perfectly fine."

"Why are you carting around an entire library? Did you have all this crap in your car?" He lifted a book to read the title and then cleared his throat before putting it back down. "Well, I'm going back to work."

I flew up, realizing my books were on display, and made quick work of gathering them together to get them into my room asap. That was how Dmitry found me when he opened his bedroom door—on my hands and knees kicking, shoveling and brushing books out of the hallway and into the privacy of my new room as quickly as I could.

His room was across the hall from mine and I'm sure I looked lovely, ass out, on all fours, surrounded by erotic novels and wearing the red-faced shame only a way-too-old-to-be-a-virgin could possess when her guilty pleasure was on full display before a house full of men.

My thick glasses were sliding down my nose, and I felt Dmitry standing behind me. I looked over my shoulder to see if I was right. Of course I was right. I could always sense Dmitry.

The little squeak I let out was embarrassing enough by itself. The position I realized I'd frozen in—on elbows and knees, ass in the air, was mortifying. I was suddenly reminded of the time I saw an ape at the zoo offering herself...never mind.

Dmitry said nothing. He just stepped back into his room and shut the door.

Konstantin let out an awkward *oof*, adding to my horror by letting me know that I'd had quite an audience for the whole Kerrigan Tran shit-show.

Struggling to my feet, I kicked the rest of my things into my room, ducked in behind them, and shut the door—a little too hard—behind me. Maybe I could stay in there and never come out.

I leaned against the door and focused on normalizing my breathing.

"Well, that could have gone better," I mumbled aloud.

The guys already thought I was a complete incompetent moron at my job. Because I was. They also thought I was small, scrawny and weak. Because, again, I was. They'd just learned I was a major klutz as well.

And Dmitry had to be home to witness that. I'd had the biggest crush on Dmitry since the moment I'd laid eyes on him—through my Coke bottle lenses.

3

It was so childish and stupid. A crush was a silly thing to have as an adult especially since I was too chicken shit to let him know how I felt. My grandmother, may she rest in peace, would've tactfully told me to shit or get off the pot. Approach the man, speak your mind, and get your answer or move it along. I had absolutely zero intention of doing any of that. Dmitry was a real life hero and I was a clumsy nerd who broke my glasses a couple times a year and either walked around with my arms out in front of me feeling my way around or held them together with electrical tape until I was able to afford a new pair.

Even though I had no intention of taking my crush on Dmitry to any level other than admiring him from afar, the damned crush remained. Instant and ever-present, my attraction hadn't faded one iota since I began working at P.O.L.A.R. If anything, it'd grown increasingly stronger. For some reason, I couldn't stop making an idiot out of myself in front of him, either. It was degrading. And the real reason I would have preferred living in my car.

With him across the hall from me, I was bound to see him even more often than I already did. I didn't need that. It was only a matter of time before I said or did the next incredibly stupid or appallingly embarrassing thing. At least living in my car, I had the chance to recover from job related screwups at night—alone in my own plastic and faux leather sanctuary.

I shoved a book away from me and thumped my head against the door. "Idiot."

The sound of rolling waves drew me away from the door and across the room to the large window I'd opened earlier. One thing that the house had that my car didn't, was an absolutely spectacular view. Beyond the beach, for as far as I could see, was the beautiful turquoise waters of the Atlantic and bright blue expanse of Florida sky. Breathtaking.

It also was a reminder of how lucky I was. Of all the places to be assigned a job, I had the good fortune to be sent to Sunkissed Key. Sand, sun, a constant bevy of shirtless men, and umbrella drinks at beach bars that a girl who lived out of her Honda Civic couldn't often afford. It was heaven.

I just had to get my head out of the metaphorical sand and get my toes in the literal sand. I could go down to the beach and get ideas for my next book as I watched all the men run around. Maybe it'd be just what the doctor ordered to get my mind off Dmitry.

I pushed my glasses up and studied the inside of my new bedroom door. To get to the beach, I'd have to travel through the house and possibly run into some of the team. They might even joke about my latest clumsy maneuver or my trashy book collection. Was it worth it?

Out the window, down on the beach, a male volleyball game was starting up. Well, that made up my mind for me. I grabbed my notebook and a pen before darting out of my room and down the stairs as fast as I could.

"Where's the fire?" Serge called out from the kitchen.

"Volleyball!" And getting away from your hot bear brother! I groaned and let the door slam behind me.

Slipping my shoes off, I left them near the back door as I sank my toes into the sand and started the short trudge to find a good spot to plant myself and watch the game.

DMITRY

I stepped out of my bedroom glaring at the closed door across the hall. That door had been ajar until quite late the night before. The room's new occupant, Kerrigan, had stayed down at the beach all evening. She sat in the sand watching some locals play at tossing a ball over a net for hours while scribbling in a notebook. She always had a notebook with her. Not always the same one, either. Then, as if that wasn't bad enough, she'd fallen asleep right there on the beach.

She was small and vulnerable. There was no way I could take my eyes off her. I'd had to stay at the window for hours looking after her and making sure nothing happened to her until she woke up—way past eleven—and decided to head back in. I'd lost sleep watching her from the window.

Downstairs in the kitchen, I yawned as I made myself some oatmeal and honey. Bears needed their sleep. Sleep was very important and I didn't like to miss it for anything. Grumbling, I poured myself a second cup of coffee and tossed it back on one swallow.

"Who pissed in your Wheaties?" Serge strolled in, looking refreshed and well rested. Bastard.

I was only half listening to Serge because just then, I heard Kerrigan's bedroom door open upstairs and her soft, light footsteps pad down the stairs and toward us. Her jet black hair was pulled back in its normal ponytail, and she entered the kitchen with a beaming smile on her face. Fake, but almost convincing. "Good morning."

Serge smiled back at her and nodded to the cabinet with the coffee cups. "Morning. Get yourself some coffee."

"Oh, no, it makes me jittery. I'll just grab a banana or something."

I ran my eyes over her lithe figure and readjusted myself in my seat. She was sexy as hell. But, would a banana be enough? I had half a mind to make her some oatmeal. She needed a real meal.

"How'd you sleep?" Serge leaned against the counter and folded his arms over his chest. "It had to be better than sleeping in that little car of yours."

Her eyes darted to me and then back to Serge. "I didn't mind the car, but I have to admit, it was nice to be able to fully stretch out."

"I'm sure."

"Well, I'm going to go for a quick swim before work." She backed away. "Bye."

I winced as she tripped over a chair and bumped into the wall. She giggled and her face flushed pink before she turned and hurried away. I gritted my teeth and shook my head. Maybe I needed to follow her—for protection. She was a bit of a hazard to herself.

"How did you sleep, Dmitry? Better, I would think." Serge smirked at me knowingly before walking out of the kitchen.

I growled. His remark told me that he knew I hadn't been sleeping at home lately. What choice did I have, though? Kerrigan seemed to have no regard for her personal safety. She'd been sleeping in her car with the windows open a crack. I had no choice but to watch over her every night. Why no one else thought it was necessary to look out for her was beyond me.

She made me nervous as hell. I never knew what she was going to do next and I felt like I was watching her with baited breath, waiting to derail her next near-catastrophe.

I thought I'd find relief with her moving into the P.O.L.A.R. house, but so far it had gotten worse. When she finally did come in from the beach last night, I'd been hyper-aware the entire night that she was just across the hall. So close I could almost reach out and touch her.

Touching her was a concept I'd been fighting since the moment I'd met her. The very second I first laid eyes on her, I'd wondered what it would be like…

I set my coffee down a little too hard and shattered the mug. As I cleaned up the mess, I focused on clearing my head. I had work to do. I needed to concentrate. Thankfully, we hadn't had any big cases since Kerrigan had started working for us. I didn't think I'd be any good to the team until I figured out how to sort out what was happening in my brain. And body.

"Hey, brother." Konstantin raised his brows. He was standing propped against the doorway. "You look like shit."

I finished throwing away the pieces of shattered mug. "Thanks."

"It wouldn't have anything to do with our newest roomie, would it?"

I glared at him before tossing the dirty towel down the laundry chute and walking out the back door. I ignored his question.

Unable to resist, I followed Kerrigan's sweet scent down to the beach and watched as she swam in the ocean. She was too far out to be able to see me. Too far out for my comfort. I had half a mind to swim out there and drag her closer to shore.

She was a good swimmer, though. I watched as she glided through the water, cutting a strong path under waves and coming back up on the other side of them. She seemed to be a different person out there. She was far more clumsy on land.

Still, my heart was in my throat the entire time I kept watch. No one had ever gotten me wound so tightly before. Kerrigan had me genuinely scared that she was going to trip and land on an open switchblade, or something equally as freaky. And, I felt it my obligation to keep her safe.

Her clothes were piled up nearby and I saw the notebook she was never without peeking out from under them. Curiosity niggled at me, but I ignored both the curiosity and my bear. He was itching to get out and go for a swim with Kerrigan. He wanted to brush against her, feel her silky skin, and roll through the crashing waves with her. He loved swimming anyway, but the thought of swimming with Kerrigan took the pastime to a whole new level.

Even though Kerrigan knew all about shifters, she'd never actually seen my bear. Most humans never came face to face with a polar bear. They might see one from afar in a zoo once or twice in their lifetime, but the size of a shifter animal was massive compared to a non-shifter animal.

When I noticed Kerrigan start to swim in, I climbed to my feet and headed back toward the house. She didn't need to know I was watching her.

KERRIGAN

To say that I wasn't qualified to work for P.O.L.A.R. would be a gross understatement. I was trained to work as an office assistant, but I'd never worked in an office where every call that came in could literally mean life or death. What if I screwed up? The stuff mattered. I had to take calls from the main office and send the guys out on location to wherever they were needed. Sounded easy, but when the office called, it was hectic. Messages were loud and rushed and I panicked.

Knowing that I was responsible for fielding calls containing critical instructions left me wound tighter than a winch pulling a two ton truck. I was a wreck. People's lives depended on my accuracy and I wasn't reliable enough for that.

Every workday, I bounced back and forth from one side of the office to the other, organizing everything I could and making myself as busy as possible. I wanted to be useful, but I also wanted to mask the fact that I'd scored the job because my mother was mated to a higher up in the organization.

It didn't help my nerves any that most of the guys in the unit hung out in the office when they weren't out on a job. They sat around, talking or horsing around, or doing whatever else they did. They kept the air conditioning set so low that I had to wear a winter jacket and they were always in the way. Not that I had any right to complain. They were the heroes, the ones actually making a difference in this world. I felt honored to be in their presence.

The enormous pressure, though! At any moment a life or death call could come in and they were all going to be there watching me, judging me. It tied my stomach in knots. I would've quit and let them find a more qualified dispatcher if I didn't desperately need the job. Of course, there was a very real possibility I'd be fired.

Dmitry was my biggest problem. He was always somewhere nearby. He stayed in a back office, but it didn't make a difference. Knowing he was so close was giving me a perpetual tremor. It was only a matter of time before I was revealed as a bumbling buffoon and it would no doubt happen right in front of him. He'd never understand. Already I was a bundle of nerves compared to his calm stoicism. I could never tell what he was thinking, but when his attention turned to me, I had a strong feeling it wasn't anything good. Whenever our eyes met, there was something strained about his expression, like I gave him heartburn.

The guys were sitting around discussing M4 versus M4A1 carbine weapons, whatever those were, when the phone rang. All eyes turned to me. My heart rate skyrocketed and I took a deep breath before answering. "P.O.L.A.R."

"Police scanner 411. 560 at 348 Second Street." The line clicked off in my ear.

Scribbling on my notepad, I stared at the numbers I'd written down for a second and then up at the guys. Even Dmitry had stepped out of the office to look at me expectantly.

"Um… Code 548 at 360 Second Street." That was right. Wasn't it? I looked at my notepad and nodded. "Yeah. 360 Second Street."

Serge appeared, slipping a handgun into his side holster. "548. Strap up. Let's go."

I watched as they all slipped guns onto holsters, horror filling my gut. I wanted to shout at them to stop—wait—let me call back and double check to make sure I'd gotten it right, but it was too late. They were already out of the door.

I ran my hands down my face and blew out a huge sigh. I didn't have a good feeling about this. What was a code 548 anyway, and why did it require guns?

"Shit."

The back door to the office opened a few seconds later, and Hannah appeared. She took one look at me and frowned. "What's wrong, Kerrigan?"

I must have looked like I felt. I'd already been fighting the urge to cry, but there was something about having someone ask you that question that made the tears inevitable. Still, I fought them. "Nothing. I'm okay."

She shook her head. "No you're not. Spill."

"I suck at this job. I know it; the guys know it. I think I may have just sent them to the wrong address, but I can't remember. It's too stressful for me, but I can't quit. I tried for weeks to find another job before this one and I only got hired here because my mom's mate pulled strings." The tears were flowing now. I reached for the box of tissues and blew my nose. "I spent so many years in school and I'm useless."

She came over to me and wrapped me in a hug. "Oh, sweetie. It's okay. Let it out."

As if I had a choice. There was no keeping it in. "The guys hate me. I know it. I'm so bad at this. I'm going to get someone killed."

"No, you're not. You'll learn. You're going to get better at it and things will be fine. It's not an easy job, taking calls from the main office. I filled in a few times. It's hard to keep up with them. You'll be a pro in no time, Kerrigan."

I didn't buy it. I was going to be fired before I ever got the chance to improve. Then, I'd hear about it from my mom—how embarrassing it was to have a daughter who was virtually incompetent and how her mate had gone through all the trouble of getting me the job in the first place. Talk about feeling like a complete failure at life.

"Maybe you should take the day off. You know, a mental health day. I could come with you? We could do a girl's day. We'll get a couple frozen margaritas and get our 'girl talk' on."

"It's ten in the morning."

She laughed. "It's never too early for frozen margaritas and girl talk with a friend."

I slid a tissue under my glasses and wiped at my eyes. I hadn't heard her call me a friend before, and at that moment, I really needed a friend. "Maybe we could go after work? I can't afford to be docked any hours right now."

"Okay. Tonight. I'm buying. I'll see if I can get Megan to come, too. If I can pry her away from Roman for a few hours. It'll be so fun!"

I pictured Dmitry rushing to possibly the wrong address with a gun drawn. "I hope I still have a job by then." Or did I? I wasn't so sure. Half of me would feel relieved to be fired.

She laughed and gave me a knowing look. "Okay. Just don't drive yourself crazy in here, Kerrigan. What you're doing is important work, yes, but not as important as your sanity."

"That's implying that I have any sanity."

She laughed. "Do you?"

Fighting a grin, I shook my head. "Not really."

4

DMITRY

*W*e entered the home, guns drawn. A 548 was code for an armed home invasion. 360 Second Street was a lovely little cottage owned by a sweet, elderly, retired couple. When we kicked in the front door and rushed the place dressed in full tactical gear, they had been seated at the breakfast table staring calmly at the morning waves while enjoying their Earl Grey and soft-boiled eggs.

The couple, Mr. and Mrs. Fuller, were so shocked that Mrs. Fuller fainted dead away. Mr. Fuller tried to fight us off using his tea cup and cane. Serge suffered a minor burn and a good whack to the side of the head.

In the end, we'd stayed to repair the door and apologize profusely. The real crime had been a simple B&E at 348 Second Street. Fortunately, the local police officers had handled the situation just fine without us.

I was torn. Part of me wanted to strangle Kerrigan. We were highly trained specialists. A fuck up like that made us look like first rate idiots. Since she'd started working at the office, we looked like idiots more and more often. The other part of me was itching to get back to her to make sure she was safe and hadn't burned down the office, with herself inside.

The guys weren't torn. They were one hundred percent pissed off at Kerrigan. Well, not Alexei. He thought the whole thing was hilarious.

Serge was fuming. "This can't happen again. The office said we had to have her, but if this keeps happening, I'm going to be forced to request a replacement. That girl's a liability."

I balled my hands at my sides and took a deep breath. He wasn't wrong. He had a job to do, too, and if a link in our chain wasn't holding its weight, someone could get hurt—or killed. It was Serge's job to make sure all links functioned. Still, I didn't like him talking about Kerrigan like that.

"How many times are we going to screw up because of her? What's going to happen when someone get injured because she can't take a simple phone message and dispatch us to the correct location?"

I growled. "Enough. We're all upset. We get it."

"I'm not. I just got to see Serge get his ass kicked by a geriatric." Alexei laughed. "Today is the best day I've had since we arrived. I think we should give the woman a raise."

Maxim snorted a laugh through his nose, but his words rang true. "It's not fucking funny, though. Mrs. Fuller could've had a heart attack and died."

I gritted my teeth and stared out the front window. "Yeah, well, she didn't."

Serge pointed a finger at me. "Teach your girlfriend how to do her job or she's gone, Dmitry."

I growled again at Serge and glared. "She is not my girlfriend, and last I checked, you're the boss. Shouldn't you have trained her better?"

Gauntlets thrown down, we drove the rest of the way back to the office in a tense silence. When we parked the van outside of the building, everyone dispersed. Roman headed toward Megan's, Serge headed towards the house, probably in search of his mate, Hannah. Konstantin, Alexei, Maxim and I went back into the office.

The silence inside was painful. Kerrigan sat at her desk with her eyes down. She already knew she'd sent us to the wrong place. I could feel the tension and humiliation rolling off of her. I sat down at the desk next to hers and sighed. She had to do better at taking down the calls from the main office. Someone had to show her.

"When the main office calls, you need to be fast. They're abrupt because they're dispatching hundreds of calls every hour to all parts of the world. You can't take your time."

Her shoulders were tense, her eyes still down. "I know."

"It's not hard. Not once you get the hang of it."

She nodded. "Okay."

Feeling frustrated, I growled. "They're going to fire you if you keep sending us to the wrong place, Kerrigan."

She stood up abruptly and looked over my shoulder. She never made eye contact if she could help it. Not with me, anyway. "I need to take care of this filing."

I stood up, towering over her, and shrugged. I wasn't sure what else to say to her. I locked myself in the back office, to get away from her. I didn't know what it was, but she drove me fucking crazy in every way. I wanted to shake her and comfort her and argue with her and kiss her.

Her feelings seemed to be so delicate and I was terrible at subtlety and tact. She probably needed some kindness and encouragement—two things I was unable to provide to anyone. I sensed that something else might be wrong with her. Something underlying that was eating away at her and keeping her mind preoccupied. I really wanted to ask her about it.

That wasn't my place, though. She was shy and sensitive and her cry reflex was near the surface. I wasn't good with crying women. I was a cold-blooded killer, not a priest. I didn't comfort people. The way I solved problems was by killing bad guys. My soul was too dark to pretend that I could make someone as gentle as Kerrigan feel better about whatever was troubling her.

None of it mattered. I was only on Sunkissed Key to do my job. Once the main office decided we'd served our penance in this blazing inferno, we'd get to go back home and I'd put Florida behind me. I'd never have to think about it again and the only thing I'd leave behind in this hell hole is perspiration.

Still, I found my mind straying to Kerrigan. It was impossible not to, her scent, her little sounds, they all permeated the walls that separated us and jumbled my senses. She kept sniffling. She was crying.

I wasn't capable of remedying a situation like that so, instead, I made myself remain in the back office. I wasn't her hero. I was no one to her.

5

KERRIGAN

*S*haring a bathroom with any man could be a challenge, but sharing a bathroom with a handful of men who regularly shifted into massive polar bears was truly an experience. I had to clean the place before I showered. The thought of Alexei using the shower before I did made me cringe. Like the rest of the guys in the unit, he was all male and I tried not to let my mind wander to the pastimes he might have indulged in while enjoying his bathroom time. And allowing myself to think about Dmitry and I sharing the same shower stall, albeit at different times, was a definite no-go.

I went straight home as soon as my shift ended. No one else was home, so I was able to snag the bathroom for myself. After scrubbing it, I set my stuff up inside and then took a nice, long shower. I took my time washing my hair and shaving, using the shower as therapy to wash the day away. When I was finished, I moisturized and brushed my teeth before wrapping a towel around me tightly and opening the door.

Dmitry stood in the hall just outside the bathroom, his mouth slightly ajar. He looked as though he was in a trance as his eyes traveled down my body and back up to my face.

I felt myself blush from head to toe and wasted no time side stepping him to get away from him. Besides still feeling humiliated about the earlier work incident, I was in a towel in front of the man I couldn't stop crushing on. I wanted to crawl in a hole and never come out. I hurried into my room, slamming the door behind me, then leaned against it and blew out a rough breath.

Barely a second passed before someone knocked at my door. "Sorry. I, uh, just needed the bathroom."

I squeezed my eyes shut and covered my face with my hands. "No problem."

"Yeah, okay."

I groaned and pushed away from the door. Why was it impossible to get Dmitry off my mind? I tried as I looked through my clothes deciding what to wear, but the effort was futile. It wasn't the gentle scolding he'd given me at the office that kept playing through my head, either. It was the sizzling look he'd given me just then as his eyes had devoured me in the hallway.

Did he find me attractive? Maybe a little? As hot as he was, he could have any supermodel in the world. He probably had. There was no way he was attracted to a skinny four-eyed woman with no hips and itty bitty titties.

I chose an emerald green maxi dress that fell to my ankles and sported a halter top with a lowcut back. I hadn't worn it for a few years, but it was the sexiest dress I owned and it complimented my black hair and the slight yellowish undertones of my complexion.

Once I had it on, I ran my hands over the lines of my panties. Eww, that wouldn't do. Thinking of the heroines in my stories, and feeling a little wild and uninhibited, I slipped off my panties. I pretended Dmitry did find me attractive, that when his eyes had raked over me out in the hall, he'd been memorizing how I looked—fresh from the shower wearing nothing but a towel—to use as fodder for his spank bank. My thoughts easily escalated from there into erotica land, dreaming up and plotting out ten different scenarios.

Not wanting to waste the creative juices, I sat down and my pen flew over the paper as started quickly jotting the ideas down. Before I knew it, the sun had set and someone was knocking on my door.

19

I sat back. The notebook in front of me was filled with scenes that should've made me blush. Instead, I was all hot and bothered. Light beads of sweat had formed between my breasts and I felt almost dizzy with arousal. It was insane, but Dmitry was a helluva muse.

When I opened the door, Hannah stood on the other side with a friendly grin. She took one look at me and whistled. "Well, look at you."

I fanned myself with my hands and smiled back at her, the stress from the early part of my day pretty much forgotten. "Ready?"

She nodded. "What were you doing in there? You look dewy. Normally, as a non-shifter I'm practically frostbitten in this house. More blue than dew, you know?"

I laughed. I did know. "I was just doing a little writing. So, where are we going tonight?"

She gave me an inquisitive look, but let it go. "Mimi's Cabana. It's a little tiki bar on the east side of the island. Mimi makes the best margaritas in Florida, I swear."

The door across the hall opened and Dmitry stepped out. When he gazed over at me, his eyes did that smoldery thing again. I looked away quickly, instantly aware of the fact that I was pantiless, and it was too late to run back into my room and change.

"Hey, Dmitry. We're heading over to Mimi's Cabana for a girl's night out. Doesn't Kerrigan look stunning?"

I didn't wait to hear his answer, instead racing down the stairs to the first floor as fast as I could and stumbling down the last two. Before I fell flat on my face, I was caught by a rough grip on my upper arms. My head snapped around. Dmitry, quick as lightning, had slipped past Hannah to catch me.

He was closer to me than he'd ever been—touching me for Christ's sake—and my body responded in the extreme. His eyes were almost completely black, pupils dilated. His nostrils flared and his grip on my arms tightened.

"Whoa! Way to be fast on your feet, D." Hannah moved past us and blew out a sharp breath. "She almost snapped her neck there."

I was suddenly aware of the moisture pooling between my thighs, my heaving chest, and my tightening nipples. I was in a heightened state of arousal and wanted to climb Dmitry like he was a tree. My throat was dry so I licked my lips and raised my eyes to his.

He just set me on my feet and stepped away, though. "Careful."

I deflated. I was a mess.

Hannah rested her hand on my shoulder and grunted. "You've got it bad, sister."

Was I that obvious? I dropped my face into my hands and groaned. "I need a drink."

6

DMITRY

"*F*ucking hell." I walked straight out of the house and down to the ocean, stripping out of my clothes along the way. I waded into the water and, once I was far enough out, shifted.

I continued swimming farther out, letting the cool water sooth my raging bear. He dove under and swam a lap before coming back up to bob in place. Kerrigan's scent was still clinging, burned into our brains. The sweet aroma of her arousal had been wafting out of her room for hours, but getting smacked in the face with it while being inches away from her was something completely different.

My bear wanted to drag her into our room and devour her, savor every morsel of her sweetness, pleasure her in every way imaginable. He wanted to make her ours.

And, it wasn't just my bear wanting those things. I had the same thoughts. After the physical contact of catching her from falling, they intensified. Touching her bare skin had been an electric shock of awareness. She'd felt it, too. I'd seen her skin flush, heard her heartrate increase and scented her arousal. I'd watched in fascination as her tongue flick out over her pink lips.

And now she was headed to a bar. Where people would see her. In a dress that exposed her bare back and accentuated her slender, waiflike figure. The slight swell of her breasts were there, for any man to see.

My bear tossed his head back and let out a wild roar. He didn't want anyone else looking at her silky skin.

Still, I stayed in the water. I was in control of my desires, mostly, and I wouldn't just cave to them when it came to Kerrigan. She was innocent. I was sure of that. I could feel it, her purity, her naivete. She was untouched and, and I damned sure wasn't the man to waste herself on.

On the other hand, someone could touch her. A man. The thought of another man touching her was enough to spike my blood pressure to a boiling rage. So much for being in control. Before I could stop myself, I was racing back to the shore. I shifted and dressed, still dripping wet.

Mimi's Cabana wasn't too far. Running, I made it there in under five minutes. I barely managed to refrain from bursting in and letting a roar rip from my throat as a warning to every swinging richard in the place to stay the fuck away from my Kerrigan. But I did manage to refrain. Instead, I paused at the front door and took a few deep breaths before calmly opening the door and glancing around.

Kerrigan was at the bar with Hannah and Megan on either side of her, sipping a frozen margarita. She reached up and tucked her long, black, silky hair behind her ears. It was the first time I'd seen it down. Like she could sense me, her eyes moved directly to me and her mouth formed a little O of surprise.

Time seemed to stand still as we stared at one another. What now? I didn't want to interrupt her girl's night, and I certainly didn't want to start something with Kerrigan that I couldn't finish. Fuck, I needed to leave her alone. I stepped backwards, back out of the bar, and headed to the house. I had no business thinking of her, let alone acting on any of those thoughts. She didn't belong to me, and a good thing, too. I'd ruin her.

I made myself go back to my room and stay there. It wasn't easy, but I had to. I was neither a good man nor a safe man—not for a woman like Kerrigan. There was nothing about me that suited a gentle woman like Kerrigan.

I stripped and climbed into bed. I wasn't tired. I figured I'd lie there and listen to the ocean until Kerrigan got close enough to the house that I could tune into her.

A few hours passed before she came back home. She went straight to her bedroom and I listened as her dress hit the floor and her mattress springs squeaked faintly as she crawled into bed. Within minutes, she was asleep.

It soothed me to know she was so close and no longer sleeping in her car, but it didn't stop me from being concerned about her safety. I listened to her steady breathing and found myself nodding off a little bit later. I woke a few hours later to the sound of Kerrigan talking in her sleep. It was the whisper of my name on her lips that had me sit up straight in bed. In her dreams she was murmuring my name—breathless and strained. I pictured her neck muscles stretched taut, her head thrown back and her spine arched as the dream took her. My name.

Sweet Kerrigan was having a dream about me. From the sound of it, it was a good dream. I paced the room, fists balled at my sides. I wanted to go to her, but that was a bad idea. A very bad idea. Terrible.

I had to cool off. The sounds were louder to my sensitive ears in the hallway, but I made it down the stairs and outside in less than a minute. Jogging down the beach and into the water, I swam far out into the sea hoping to cool off and calm down enough to get a few more hours sleep.

It took forever to regain control and by the time the sun rose, I was exhausted. I felt like I'd been whipped and beaten then drawn and quartered. It was all I could do to make it to work. Fortunately, it was Saturday and Kerrigan was off. I was hoping I could hide out in the back office and catch up on some Z's. No such luck.

A call came in about a hostage situation involving a shifter in Miami. A little out of our way, but right up our alley. Despite each and every man on our team being a deadly and highly trained operative, we each had our own unique skill set. Terminations were mine. I was a crack shot and skilled at virtually any weapon, but I was best at hand to hand. I was the assassin.

So, when a particularly out of control alligator shifter was rampaging and threatening the lives of a woman and her children, I did what I had to do. I didn't love it. But it was a necessary evil. Taking out shifters who were threatening and posing a deadly risk to humans sometimes included an odd twist. After the fact, the victims sometimes looked at you as though *you* were the villain.

The alligator shifter had been seconds from snapping her young son's neck, but she was screaming mad that I'd killed the fucker. It didn't take much to deduce that mom was high on something and that, whatever it was, he had been her supplier. Hell, maybe she did love him. What did I know about love? I just knew my job. And I'd done it. I'd neutralized the threat and saved the kid's life.

It didn't matter to Mom, though. She screamed and wailed and called me a heartless monster. According to her, there was a special place in hell for me. I didn't doubt that.

Her screeching could be heard over her child's sobs and continued on even after the police arrived to clean up the messy scene.

The ride back to the island was quiet. No one wanted to talk about what had just gone down. None of us had the stomach for small talk.

Kerrigan was on my mind more than ever. I kept seeing her shy features transposed onto that woman's screaming face. Surely, Kerrigan would have been appalled if she knew what I'd just done. I pictured Kerrigan with a horrified expression—crying and screaming. Telling me to get away from her, telling me there was a special place in hell for me. There was an ugly side to our job that none of us loved, or wanted to rehash. We did what had to be done.

Feeling like the weight of the world was on my shoulders, I chose not to go back to the office. I was in no mood to plaster a fake smile on and hang with the guys. Despite knowing it probably wasn't the best choice, I went home. Not to see Kerrigan, or so I told myself. She probably wouldn't even be home. I'd just close myself in my room and forget everything.

In truth, deep down, I hoped she was home.

7

KERRIGAN

I'd quickly decided that Saturdays in the P.O.L.A.R. house were my favorite. I was off on Saturdays but the guys usually went in to the office, and Hannah along with them. So, I could just hang out and spend lazy alone time without worrying about bumping into anyone who was ticked at me or disappointed in my job performance. I spent the morning at the dining room table, writing until my hand cramped. Then, I watched an episode of Iron Chef in the living room before making a bologna sandwich for lunch and retreating to my room. I was just finishing my sandwich and thinking about going out for a swim when I heard the door slam downstairs.

I knew who it was because the hair on the back of my neck instantly stood on end. Dmitry. I hadn't seen him since the night before when he'd appeared in the bar, took one long look at me, and then turned and fled. Probably didn't like what he saw, and decided to drink elsewhere.

I left my bedroom door open and was standing just inside, waiting for him to come up the stairs. Maybe I should have closed the door and minded my own business, but something in the air felt different.

Dmitry hurried up the stairs and slammed his bedroom door shut behind him. Just that quick glimpse of him made my pulse race. His face had been drawn and his expression even darker than usual. It wasn't my business. I should have just closed my door and let it go.

The image of his haunted face was too much, though. It touched me to the core. My feet felt like lead as I dragged myself across the hallway pausing just outside of his door. I was being an idiot. He didn't need to be comforted by me, no matter what was bothering him. He probably wanted to be left alone.

Still, I lifted my arm and gently tapped on his door. When it swung open a few seconds later, I gasped. He stood tall but something about him looked...broken. "Dmitry? Are you okay?"

I'd been expecting him to slam the door in my face or ignore me or give me a dirty look and tell me to get lost. I was no one to him. Just the incompetent, nerdy dispatcher who was a living anti-nepotism argument. I couldn't blame him for not liking me. Instead, he shocked the hell out of me when he reached out and snatched me into his arms.

He hugged me against his chest and in the split second before his mouth claimed mine, I took every sensation in—his muscled abs against my worn t-shirt, his smoky, fresh scent seducing me with every inhale, his blonde hair begging for my fingers to comb through it.

With my hands and arms trapped between us, palms flat against his rock hard chest, and my thighs pressed against the thick canvas of his cargo pants, it was enough to fill pages and pages in my notebook.

Then, his kiss was on my lips. Hard and urgent, Dmitry devoured me like we were on a sinking ship and this kiss was the only lifeline. He kissed me with a fierceness that was almost rough. His hands on my waist were hard and punishing, his fingertips digging into my flesh, the shadow of his beard leaving a friction burn. I loved it!

His actions had caught me so off guard that it had taken me a second to realize he was kissing me. Before I could really get into it and kiss him back, he lifted me and spun us so my back was pressed against his door. His hands caught my ass and squeezed as he kissed me harder. I gasped and my libido kicked into overdrive. Yes! Forget the rules—all of them.

I held on to his shoulders as his tongue explored my mouth. He tasted like sunshine. I moaned into his mouth as our tongues tangled. He was demanding, controlling, and almost panicked in his intensity. There was no hiding how much he wanted me. He rocked the proof into my core.

He tilted his head and kissed me deeper, stroking his tongue against mine, creating a dance that fueled every nerve ending of desire I possessed. My head was flooded with the feeling of him against me. My dreams had barely scratched the surface of what this really felt like. His body was hard and hot against mine. The smell, the taste of him, I was reeling with pleasure.

I didn't realize we'd moved until I felt his fingers at the top of my waistband. We were on his bed, with me straddling him. My knees rested on the plaid blanket of his perfectly made bed, and he was nipping and sucking kisses down my throat. It never crossed my mind that we should slow down. Or stop to think. We were both consenting adults. As far as I was concerned, full speed ahead.

I ran my fingers through his short blonde hair and held onto his head while he sucked on my collar bone. His teeth were rough, but they felt like they were nibbling away the tension I'd been holding. Like a drug, I wanted more.

Dmitry slid his hand into my panties and his long, thick finger stroked over my folds. He growled before he captured my mouth again, kissing, devouring, reddening my face with the faint stubble of his beard. Both of us were breathing raggedly as I held myself up on my knees and locked my arms around his neck.

His finger continued to stroke me, parting my folds. I was in heaven. With his other arm bracing me behind my back, he slid his finger into me, filling me. He swallowed my moans and held me tighter as I trembled against him, the sensation so amazing that I couldn't hold off an orgasm if I wanted to. My body felt as though I'd collapse at any second but he didn't stop. Holding me, peppering kisses all over my face and neck and chest, he pumped his finger in and out of me, drawing another orgasm from me before I could even recover from the first.

I couldn't hold on. I'd never felt someone else's anything inside of me and Dmitry was hitting me in all the right places. His fingers were thick and long and rough. He was not gentle and something about that pushed me straight over the edge. He pinched my nipples with his teeth as my hips worked against his hand, his palm grinding against my clit.

The third orgasm started fast and hit me like a tidal wave. I held tightly to Dmitry and bit down on his lip while his fingers continued to piston within my tightening walls. Shaking, hips bucking, the only thing that kept me from flying off of his lap was his arm locked firmly around me.

My head snapped back and I screamed out his name as my climax hit. I tasted his blood on my tongue and I should've been more concerned about that, but I was flying high. Dmitry's lips were on my throat, still. His fingers still filled me, his palm still rested against my sweet spot.

I had never felt so amazing in all my life. I wanted to tell him, but I couldn't get my mouth to work just yet. My heart slammed against my rib cage, my pulse fluttered at the base of my throat, near Dmitry's mouth. Everything felt surreal, like I'd floated into another dimension —someplace where everything was a party with rainbows and unicorns.

Reality always had a way of crashing the party, though.

Dmitry pulled his hand away suddenly and set me on unsteady feet, a foot away from him. Not meeting my eyes, he gestured towards his door. "Go on."

I didn't understand, so I just stood there like an idiot.

He turned away from me and fiddled with something on top of his dresser. "Go on back to your room, Kerrigan. I'm so sorry."

My stupid, fluttering heart that had been soaring the stratosphere suddenly crash landed at my feet. I think I kicked it as I turned and rushed out of his room. By the time I was safely shut away behind my bedroom door, I was crying big, fat tears. They rolled down my cheeks and dripped off my chin. I sat on my bed staring at the door hoping he'd been joking and was going to come rushing in at any second, sweep me into his arms, and carry me back to his bed. Instead, his door shut with a loud slam. I flopped back onto the bed and stared at the ceiling.

I had no clue what had just happened. Had I done something wrong? My body was still floating on air from the first and only orgasm given to me by someone other than myself. My body clearly hadn't gotten the memo that shortly thereafter, I'd been curtly dismissed. Not even dismissed. Kicked out. With an apology too, as though the whole thing was an accident.

I choked back a sob and dragged a pillow over my face. I felt devastated. Humiliated.

The more I racked my brain, the more confused I felt. I knew anger would come eventually and I welcomed it. It was far easier to deal with than humiliation.

8

DMITRY

I'd behaved unforgivably. After kicking Kerrigan out of my room, I spent the rest of the weekend locked inside, berating myself, ashamed of what I'd done to her and how I'd done it. Well, I was sorry for how rough I'd been. I couldn't deny that every time I closed my eyes, I pictured her lithe body and her soft moans of pleasure. It was torture. The memories of her crying out my name at the height of ecstasy played through my head like a porno on a loop. I knew it had been wrong, though—all wrong.

She deserved better. She was high-strung and fragile, easily reduced to tears. I'd been rough and then kicked her out. Worse, I'd heard her crying and smelled her tears. I knew she was upset and I wanted to go to her and comfort her, but anything I might do or say would only make the situation worse. I didn't know how to comfort someone—anyone. For someone like Kerrigan, I was a problem not a solution.

There was another reason for staying away from her—the main reason. She called to my bear like no other person on the planet. I wasn't convinced I could control myself around her and not grab her and do it all over again if the opportunity presented.

My bear had nearly ripped me to shreds trying to claim her the first time, the woman he was referring to as his mate. I supposed she was. She had to be based on the feelings I was having for her. But it wasn't fair to her to act on such things. Fate was cruel to pair me with Kerrigan. She deserved so much better. So, while my bear demanded his mate, I refused to allow it.

Instead, I avoided her. It was hell, but it was necessary. I waited until she was asleep and I had no chance of an accidental encounter before I snuck out to eat and swim. Like a complete coward, I even climbed out of my window to go to the office and to use the bathroom. I wasn't proud but it had to be done. I kept picturing her sorrowful, tear-stained face and that gave me impetus to continue to avoid her.

It was almost laughable that I, a polar bear—the largest, fiercest, most dangerous bear in existence, was spinelessly shaking in his fur at the thought of facing a tiny, 100-lb woman.

By sheer coincidence, I'd also ended up avoiding the rest of the P.O.L.A.R. unit. When Monday morning finally rolled around, I wondered if the team would know what a monster I'd been. Maybe Kerrigan had spilled to Hannah and Hannah in turn to Serge who told the rest of the unit. Maybe Kerrigan hated me. It would make everything easier if she hated me.

As I stepped into the office that morning, and the guys treated me as always, no questioning looks or smartass remarks, though, I knew she hadn't told a soul. But Kerrigan's desk was empty. I stared at it for a few seconds too long, when Serge came in and caught me.

"She's sick, I guess. She called this morning to let me know she couldn't make it in today."

"She *called* you?"

He frowned. "Yeah, she hasn't been out of her room all weekend. I guess she's been sick the whole time. I don't know. Hannah's taking her soup, or something. Looks like we get a day free from looking like completely incompetent idiots."

I growled under my breath at Serge's insult to Kerrigan, but there was nothing I could say. What I'd done to her was worse than Serge's implied insult. I sauntered to the back and sank into an office chair.

"You look bright and chipper today." Alexei followed me and sat across from me. "This wouldn't have anything to do with our missing dispatcher, would it?"

I scowled at him. "Don't start with me, Alexei. I'm in no mood."

"No? Whyever not? A lover's quarrel with everyone's favorite Disney Princess Mulan, perhaps?"

I knew he was attempting to push my buttons, and I should have ignored him, yet I didn't. "Mulan is Chinese not Vietnamese, dumbass. And furthermore, fuck you."

"Me? Fuck me? Please, we all know it's not me you want to fuck."

I was up and dragging him across the room before either of us could blink. I slammed him into the wall so hard we both went through it and fell into the front offices where the rest of the team was holed up. I shoved off of Alexei and stalked angrily toward the door.

"Um, excuse me? You two want to explain why the fuck you just remodeled the place?" Serge gestured towards the chalky mess that had been a wall seconds earlier. Alexei was on top of the pile of drywall pieces, a stupid grin on his face. "And why are you grinning? What did you do? You're fucking with him, aren't you? Shit, what am I saying? Of course you're fucking with him."

I ignored them all and left. I needed some air and to calm the fuck down.

I worked through every trick I'd ever learned about how to calm the animal inside as I headed toward the beach, including counting slowly to a hundred. Nothing was working. My bear was pushing to get out.

It took me a few seconds to realize that Kerrigan's scent was what was riling him so much. Her naturally delicious aroma was mixed with the acrid scent of fear and I also scented another male near her. I growled low in my throat and charged forward, teetering on the verge of a shift, more bear than man.

Down the beach, I spotted Kerrigan, her sandals in her hand, staring up at a fully dressed man, dress slacks and collared shirt, whose back was to me. Her face was contorted in worry and I could feel the anxiety rolling off of her.

Instinct told me to charge the man. He was threat and needed to be taken down. But before I could implement the maneuver, Kerrigan hung her head and stepped around him. Eyes downcast, she strode quickly toward the house, not even noticing me.

"Don't cross me, Kerrigan." The man's warning carried to me due only to the direction of the breeze and my shifter hearing. "You hand over more or you'll be paying in other ways."

Kerrigan's shoulders stiffened and she froze for a moment without looking back, before running into the house. I watched until she slipped inside and shut the door behind her.

Back down the beach, the man was already walking briskly away, whistling the theme from Jeopardy. The picture of ease and contentment, I was pretty sure I'd just overheard a threat of some sort—possibly a blackmail attempt.

My already agitated bear eating me alive trying to get me to shift right then and there and end the fucker. Fortunately, I still had some rational brain power—enough to put two and two together. Kerrigan was in some kind of trouble. The man may have thought he had the upper hand, but what he didn't know was that Kerrigan had a small army of highly trained, lethal polar bear shifters at her back. Or that it would require only one of us to neutralize him. Me.

9

KERRIGAN

*B*ack in my room, I emptied the contents of my purse on my bed and gathered all the loose change that had fallen to the bottom. Then, I emptied the shoebox under my bed. I didn't have much. Everything went toward my student loan payments. One loan in particular. I gathered the small stack of bills in my trembling hands. It wasn't enough.

I wouldn't get my paycheck from P.O.L.A.R. until Friday. Once I did, I would have just enough to settle with Knuckles for the next month. The problem was that I didn't know how to convince him to hold off until I cashed my paycheck. But, there was no other way. I couldn't ask Serge for an advance. I hadn't even worked there long enough. Plus, I was pretty sure he hated me. They all did.

I was praying my miniscule savings would hold Nicky over until payday. I shoved the cash into an envelope and sat on the edge of my bed wondering if I was just prolonging the inevitable. How long could I hold the man off? He was getting pushier and pushier—demanding double the normal payment amount. Why? Because he could. I had no recourse. Private loans weren't governed by any laws, so he could do whatever he wanted. It hadn't taken me long to realize he was a loan shark. A greedy, evil loan shark named Nicky "Knuckles" Palermo who was known on the street as Nicky Knuckles. Unfortunately, I'd learned of his street reputation too late, after I'd already borrowed a hefty chunk of change. Now I was drowning in my biggest mistake.

I rested my head in my hands and tried to steady my erratic breathing. It wasn't easy. I was terrified and rightly so. Knuckles was getting nastier. He'd threatened me with horrible things. Breaking my kneecaps had been an early threat. Selling me into sex slavery was the latest. The threat worked because I was pretty sure he actually had the power to do it. So, with my personal safety on the line, I was willing to do whatever I could to procure and hand over double my normal payment.

The trouble was, whenever I met one of his demands, he had another, more difficult stipulation and I had no recourse. I was between a rock and a hard place. I knew I needed help, but I didn't feel right involving anyone else in my mess. Besides, I didn't have anyone else to involve.

My mom was off in Northern Russia somewhere with her mate. My father had been dead for years. I had no siblings or any other family. I'd been too busy in college, with my nose always in a textbook, to make friends or engage in social activities. After college, I'd hustled my butt off working two jobs—nightshift at a convenience store, and days writing for a small magazine. No time for social pursuits. When the magazine shut down, I lost my tiny apartment and lived out of my Honda Civic. I was lucky to have Mom's mate find me the job with P.O.L.A.R. even though it meant moving an hour away and losing the second job at the convenience store.

I was alone. Worse than alone, lonely. Oddly, before meeting Dmitry, alone and lonely weren't synonymous. Now, the loneliness was a slow burning ache.

I rubbed my tired eyes and stood up. I couldn't be bellyaching about Dmitry. Not when I had real problems to deal with. Knuckles was back to his highly effective intimidation tactics. He was a legit danger.

Whatever had happened with Dmitry was a mistake, anyway. A dumb, stupid mistake. If anyone found out, I would lose my job and right now, that was the only thing keeping Nicky Knuckles from selling me into sex slavery. I'd had to sign a strict non-fraternizing contract. After some incident that caused a big tadoo and got the team in trouble, the main office wasn't taking any chances. If I was caught dating or otherwise sharing intimate relations with any of the guys in the P.O.L.A.R. unit, I was out. And not even my mom's mate could stop it. It was bad enough that I sucked majorly at my job, I couldn't afford to be a rebellious rule-breaker, too.

My silly crush and my raging hormones had allowed me to jeopardize the house of cards that was my life. If I was out of a job and Nicky Knuckles found out, I'm pretty sure his reaction would be swift and brutal. I damned sure couldn't afford to let thoughts of Dmitry allow this precarious balance to crumble.

And I had! I'd called off sick because of what had happened with Dmitry even though I couldn't afford to be shorted a day's pay. Not only that, but I had to do better and work harder, so P.O.L.A.R. wouldn't fire me.

I pulled my hair up in a ponytail and headed back out in the direction of the team office.

Like a cruel joke from life, Dmitry was opening the front door just as I was about to. I didn't meet his eyes as I sidestepped him and rushed away. Part self-preservation, part hurt, I didn't want to see him. I never wanted to see him again. Already, as it was, I couldn't stop thinking about him.

"Kerrigan…"

I tossed a wave in his direction. "Can't talk. On my way to work."

I picked up my pace until I was running, and made it to the office in minutes. Shocking everyone, I burst into the frigidly cold building sweaty and out of breath. Serge stood up from my desk and frowned. "What are you doing here, Kerrigan?"

"Miraculously, I'm healed. And reporting for duty."

"There's no problem with you taking a sick day. We'll manage just fine. You should take the day to rest up so you're at 100% tomorrow."

I didn't meet his eyes, and simply plopped into my desk chair. "No, thanks."

He looked like he had more to say but the phone rang.

I yanked it up and brought it to my ear. "P.O.L.A.R."

Listening while a harried woman shouted numbers at me, I yelled them out to the room just as she'd yelled them to me. Slamming the phone down, I turned to the men who were all staring at me and widened my eyes. "Well?"

Alexi sported a half-grin. "That works."

Maxim nodded. "Got it."

Serge patted my shoulder with his heavy hand. "Good job, Kerrigan. Keep it up."

I stared down at my desk as they did their thing and geared up for the job. I didn't want to see if the call involved weapons or not. I just wanted to do my job and pay my debts. If I could avoid getting sold into slavery, that would be great, too.

Alexei stopped at my desk and ruffled my ponytail. "The yelling technique. I like it. Serge likes to be yelled at—keeps him in line."

Serge slapped the back of Alexei's head and shoved him towards the door. "Hannah is stopping by. Do me a favor and lock the door while the two of you are here alone."

"But not when I'm here alone?" The question was out before I could stop it.

He hesitated and frowned. "Yeah, you should lock the door when you're alone, too."

I nodded. "Sure."

It was just another reminder that I meant nothing to them. He wanted his mate safe, but it hadn't crossed anyone's mind to care about me.

I waved them off and left the door unlocked. What did it matter? The most dangerous man to me was already on the island and had my number. The second most dangerous man slept across the hall from me. I was screwed, no matter what.

10

KERRIGAN

I needed a drink, and not just one. Most of my money was going to Nicky Knuckles, but I'd seen a flyer posted at Mimi's Cabana when Hannah, Megan and I had been there on our girls' night outing that advertised dollar beers for Monday night happy hour. It was Monday and I was planning to hit those dollar drafts hard.

I headed to Mimi's straight after work. Alone. I didn't care that it might look weird to be sitting on a barstool sucking back cheap beers all by my lonesome before it was even dinnertime for the senior crowd. I truly didn't care.

The interior of Mimi's Cabana was all Polynesian themed with tiki masks, palm trees and coconuts. I was surprised Mimi hadn't carted in sand for the flooring. Mimi herself was a larger woman who wore a coconut bra and grass skirt to work daily. She had curves on top of curves, but she actually made it work. I liked her. She was all smiles and sunshine.

The dollar beers were served from 4pm to 6pm. It was a little after four thirty, so I had to get right to drowning my sorrows. I started out strong by ordering two beers from Mimi. I sat at the bar so it would be easy to get my refills when those were gone.

Dollar beer tasted a little like flat sour ginger ale without the ginger, but it was ice cold and after the first, the next went down easily. I found the more I drank, the lighter my problems became. The alcohol was numbing my weighty emotions for the moment and I was all for it. It was just the respite I needed. Beer number two had gotten warm, but I didn't care about that. When Mimi came back, I ordered two more.

"Honey, what's going on with you? I only gave you two beers to start out with because I thought you had a friend coming." Mimi poured me another but held it back. "A little slip of a thing like you shouldn't be downing so much so fast. What's got you chugalugging?"

"Men." I shook my head. "Two men, to be exact."

She pouted her thick lips and poured a fourth beer for me. "That I understand. If I wasn't working, I might join you in guzzling these things myself."

I saluted her with my Beer number three and burped. "Excuse me."

She just laughed and patted my shoulder as she wandered off to serve her other patrons. "Hold it together, honey."

Hold it together. Didn't that sound easy? I was intelligent, compassionate, well-educated. I could write a novel in under two months and be proud of it. Yet, there I was chugging back dollar beers and wondering how much longer I could balance on the tightrope I was walking.

The fourth beer was the best of all. I saw some fruity drink with a fancy umbrella served in a coconut go by and almost fell out of my chair drooling over it. Mimi noticed and grinned. "Stick to beer, honey, or you'll hate yourself in the morning."

So, I did. I had a fifth before the happy hour deadline arrived. I was wasted, anyway. I wasn't much of a drinker, but I usually held my alcohol fairly well for a woman who was a hair over five foot tall and weighed about 100 pounds soaking wet. Or, I could at least pretend to hold my alcohol. That night was different. I felt every ounce of cheap draft sloshing around in my gut, taunting me with the knowledge that it wasn't actually going to solve any of my dilemmas.

The numbed emotions were still there, just under the surface, but now I felt out of control. I swayed on my stool, which had nothing to do with the song playing in the background.

When someone sat down on the stool beside me, I paid them no mind. I was in my own world, wondering how long it would be before I could safely stand up without embarrassing the hell out of myself. Mimi had brought me a glass of water, but I needed to pee again and not another drop of was going to fit inside of me until I did.

"You drinking away all of my money, Kerrigan?"

I steadied myself by grasping the lip of the bar and digging my fingernails in. My eyes remained on the bar top. Nicky Knuckles. What the hell was he doing here? I'd already texted him that he could have my meager savings and that I'd give him the balance when I got paid. Why was he stalking me?

"Don't ignore me, sweetheart. That's not very nice."

"What do you want, Nicky?"

He wrapped his arm around my waist and leaned into me, his stale breath on my face was like a warm breeze rolling off a trash heap. "You know what I want."

I shuddered, the feeling of him so close was worse than having a slithering snake crawl over my skin. "I-I already told you when I'd have your money."

He *tsk*-ed and lightly tugged at the end of my ponytail. "I'm an impatient man. If you want me to wait until Friday, I'll need to be entertained in the meantime—in other ways."

I tried to pull away, but he was strong. "Leave me alone."

He grasped my chin between his thumb and forefinger and forced my face to turn his way. His grin was bone chilling. "Let's dance."

I tried to hold onto the bar, but it was useless. Nicky was a big man and he easily picked me up merely by scooping his arm around my waist. He put me down out of reach of the stool and bar. When I tried to pull away, I felt the room spin and he simply wrapped his arms around me and held me against his chest. My face pressed into his shirt, his sickly sweet smelling cologne made me gag and the gold chain he wore dug into the side of my cheek.

"There we go. Isn't this nice?" He ran his hands up and down my back, his grip firm. "Just a nice dance between old friends—or maybe a little more than friends."

The threat was clear. He was letting me know how easily he could overpower me and that, unless I wanted everyone to know my shameful secret, there was nothing I could do about it. I wanted to scream, to beg someone to help me get away from him, but I knew it would only make things worse for me. Even filled to the brim with liquid courage, I knew better than to try to cross Nicky. The punishment would be too severe.

His strong cologne was mixed with cigarette smoke. I could feel the prickliness of his chest hair through the silk shirt he wore. My heart hammered in my chest and I had twin death grips on each side of his shirt, fighting to stay upright. I felt like I was going to vomit.

There were other couples dancing around us to the piped in calypso music and I knew that we didn't stand out. A bar full of people around and Nicky could maul me in plain sight without anyone noticing.

"There's something you should know about me, Kerrigan. I always get what I want. Always."

"Just let me pay you on Friday. Please."

He dug his fingers into my back suddenly and then pulled away with a big smile on his face. "Thanks for the dance."

"Honey, you okay?" Mimi was right behind me, undoubtedly the real reason Nicky had let me go. "Let's get you to a chair. You can barely stand on your own, child."

I wanted to kiss Mimi I was so thankful for her. I didn't notice whether or not Nicky left. I didn't see anything else. I was too focused on putting one foot in front of the other on a relatively straight path back to the barstool. That, and trying to keep the room from spinning.

"Okay, here we go." Mimi tried to help me, but I was already wobbling like a newborn colt.

Trying to get onto the stool was a joke. I lifted one leg and the other one buckled beneath me. Before I could help it, I was going down.

11

DMITRY

*T*he job we were on—a stakeout of a suspected arsonist—had run long and I didn't make it back to the house until after six. I had a slight gnawing in my gut all due to Kerrigan. My mind kept straying to her, the strange man who'd threatened her and what kind of trouble she might be in. Planning to confront her, I went straight to her bedroom and found the door cracked. The room was empty.

I walked over to the office to see if she was still there, but she wasn't. I tried the beach and scanned the waves to see if maybe she'd gone out for a swim. She was nowhere to be seen. The gnawing in my gut was worse than ever.

Anyone seen Kerrigan?

Immediately Serge's thoughts filled my head. *Nope. Hannah said she wasn't looking too good when she saw her at the office today.*

Shit. Something was wrong. She was in some kind of trouble. But what kind, exactly?

Megan says to check Mimi's. They all talked about the happy hour deal when they were there the other night. Maybe she stopped for a drink. Everything okay? Roman's voice was laden with concern which merely served to amp my fear up even more.

I don't know yet.

I took off at a sprint towards Mimi's Cabana. I had to cross Main Street and cut down Flamingo Lane, but as soon as I got close, I could smell her. Her natural aroma was mixed with the sour scent of fear and the pickling of alcohol.

Found her.

I all but ripped Mimi's door off to get inside and what I saw incensed me and enraged my bear to the point I had to fight him to keep from an uncontrolled shift in a barroom packed with people. Kerrigan was there. So was the dickweed who'd been threatening her earlier—and he was touching her. His back was to me, but he was easy to distinguish from his clothes and stature. He had his arms around her so tightly that it looked as though he was trying to suffocate her.

Mimi, a concerned look on her face, was behind Kerrigan and while I concentrated on counting to ten before I did something stupid like rip that fucker's head off and sully Mimi's Caribbean décor with spatters of blood and chunks of flesh, he stepped back. When he did, I saw the state Kerrigan was in. So much for counting to ten. She could barely stand on her own. The fucker had to have been holding her up. Had he been trying to take advantage of her in her intoxicated state?

I was seconds from a gruesome kill when I was distracted by Mimi supporting Kerrigan and guiding her to a barstool. Kerrigan was falling backwards. Even with my shifter strength and speed, I was too far away to catch her before she hit the ground. The *thump* was painful to hear, but Kerrigan didn't seem any worse for the wear. She just hiccupped and grinned, an embarrassed pink tinge to her face.

Mimi spotted me coming and whispered to Kerrigan, "You didn't hold it together honey."

"I really tried." Kerrigan's voice was watery and I was concerned I was going to see tears.

I didn't want to *see* the tears. I heard them on occasion. Smelled them, too, but that was different. I could almost pretend they weren't real. I had a feeling I was about to be hit with a motherlode of tears. "You okay, Kerrigan?"

Her head snapped to me and, the tears I'd been expecting vanished.

Her brown eyes focused on me and she groaned as though seeing me was the thing she'd expected or wanted. "Oh."

I frowned. "Come on. Let's get you home."

She took Mimi's hand over mine and when she was on two feet again, she took a moment to steady herself. Blowing out a deep breath that smelled like beer, she nodded to herself and squared her shoulders. It would've been more convincing if she hadn't also been chewing her lower lip.

I ran my hand down my face and looked around, trying to spot the asshole who'd been touching her. He'd already slipped out. Fuck. I'd let him get away.

Kerrigan stumbled when she took her first step, but still recoiled when I held my arm out to help her. That's how it went. Getting out of the bar took forever. She took a few steps and then stumbled, but refused to accept my help. I let her go it on her own while we were in the crowd of people because I didn't want to make a scene—or any more of a scene.

As soon as we cleared the doorway, though, I swept her into my arms and carried her home. She weighed next to nothing, even while wriggling in an attempt to get down.

"You need to put me down. Right now." She hiccupped and burped at the same time, something that clearly embarrassed her. She groaned and buried her face in her hands.

"You're too drunk to walk a straight line. It'd take you until next week to get home at this rate." I cut through someone's side yard to make it home faster.

"I can walk just fine. I don't want you to carry me."

"Too bad."

"Put me down." She hiccupped again. "You...you...overgrown teddy bear."

I cocked my head at her and looked up and down Main Street before crossing it. "Excuse me?"

She sighed. "Oh, I'm sorry. I shouldn't call you names."

She was apologizing to me. She'd done nothing wrong. I was the asshole, or the overgrown teddy bear, as she'd put it.

45

"Kerrigan…"

She shook her head and hiccupped again. "I don't want to conversate with you. *Hiccup.*"

I walked the rest of the way in silence, arriving at the house faster than I wanted to. I put her down on the front steps of the house to have a few words with her privately. "I think we—"

She bent over, stumbled, hiccupped, took her shoes off, and then started weaving her way down to the beach. I watched her go, stumbling and falling two, three, times, before she settled into the sand at the edge of the water and let the tide roll over her feet. Following behind her, I was fully intent on taking advantage of her inebriated state to get her to open up and talk to me—to tell me what was wrong and why that asshat had been all over her earlier. I thought we'd finally get a chance to talk and the fact that her inhibitions were reduced by alcohol was a benefit in my mind. Okay, maybe it wasn't the most honorable plan, but I really needed to find out who the man was that had been hanging around and what the hell was going on with her. I also wanted to apologize for treating her so poorly.

My plan didn't work, though. Kerrigan had nothing to say to me.

12

KERRIGAN

I didn't want to hear a word Dmitry said. Not a word. I was still too drunk to trust myself with rational conversation. Who knew what might come out of my mouth? Besides, whatever he wanted to talk about was probably going to sting like hell. Something along the lines of, "I never should have put my hands on you. Please don't tell anyone, blah, blah."

When he sank down next to me in the sand, I didn't look over at him. I'd already spent too much time dying inside over the way he'd carried me back from Mimi's. I kicked off my sandals and then leaned back to get to my pants button.

"What are you doing?"

I stood back up and walked to the water. "Going for a swim."

I kicked out of my pants and then threw my shirt onto the small pile before wading out in the water. It was cold against my overheated skin, the sand rough under my toes. Still plenty of daylight left. I should've been embarrassed to be swimming in my bra and panties in the late afternoon on a public beach. I wasn't.

Up to my hips, up to my breasts, up to my chin. When I couldn't touch the sandy bottom of the ocean floor, I breaststroked out deeper. I'd swim across the ocean if that's what it took to get far away from

Nicky Knuckles and his slime ball threats. I even wanted to get away from Dmitry.

I swam out farther and farther until I could look back at the beach and not see him through my water-spotted glasses. Floating on my back, I stared up at the bright blue sky until my eyes burned and I had to squeeze them shut.

The alcohol was still flowing through my system, making my problems just a bit out of reach. I felt like my fingertips could just graze them, but not pull them close. They loomed, just out there on the horizon, reminding me that they would still be there when I sobered up, tomorrow, next week, maybe forever.

I was pitiful. My life was pitiful.

I held my breath and let myself sink under the water. Blowing out my breath, I sank even lower. My eyes closed, my lungs tight, I paddled my arms to keep myself under. I felt free there—cloaked. I pretended no one would be able to find me and I could float under the water and never have to worry about a thing.

No rent or mortgage, no exorbitant student loans, I'd just float in the ocean, under the waves. It wouldn't matter if I sucked at my job and no one liked me, or if the only man I'd been intimate with wanted to pretend it never happened. It wouldn't matter because the fish didn't care.

My lungs burned, but I stayed under. I didn't want to die. I just didn't want to be up top, up above the waterline. The world was too hard.

Something brushed against my leg and I felt something massive wrap around me, dragging me upwards. I didn't have to open my eyes to know what it was, who it was. Dmitry. More specifically, Dmitry's bear.

We crested the surface and I sucked in a huge breath of air and coughed.

Next to me was the largest animal I'd ever seen face to face. Snow white with a black nose and Dmitry's dark blue eyes, the bear was awesome—as in awe-inspiring. It opened its mouth and roared, revealing huge, razor-sharp teeth and a black tongue. Still, I felt no fear.

I bobbed in the water next to it and found myself smiling. I was clearly still drunk. Running my hand over its head, I felt something melt inside of me. There was pain and heartache in the real world, above water, but there were also amazing, extraordinary, incredible things. I was stroking the head of a polar bear shifter. The most beautiful polar bear I'd ever seen. He was growling while I did it, but still, he was letting me.

Then, a split-second later, the bear was gone and Dmitry was in front of me again. My hand was still stroking over his head and face.

I should probably stop petting him. Yeah.

He stared at me with a furious scowl and shook his head. "Out of the water."

I sighed. The beer buzz was still with me, strongly, but not enough to keep me from feeling down that he looked at me like that, like he hated me.

Dmitry wasted no time in wrapping his arm around my waist, and all but dragging me back to shore. When we got close enough to stand, he let me go, stepping ahead of me, but grabbed my hand to pull me after him. Wow, he had a tightly formed ass—and no tan lines. When I giggled, he glared at me over his shoulder.

His shirt and pants were in a pile next to mine and he stepped into his pants with his back still to me. He seemed to be waiting for me to do the same, but I wasn't putting my clothes back on. I wasn't ready to go back to real life just yet.

That just seemed to deepen his scowl. Especially when he turned around and saw me sitting in the sand in just my bra and panties. He threw his hands up. "What the fuck was that?"

I furrowed my brows. "What was what?"

"That! Were you trying to drown yourself?" He put his hands on his hips and glared down at me. "You went under and you didn't come back up. You about gave me a heart attack."

"You're a shifter. You'll be fine." I waved him off. "Do shifters even have heart attacks?"

It was the wrong thing to say. "Kerrigan, you can't... I forbid you to drown yourself! Jesus Christ. I can't believe I have to say that to you. You can't just swim out and go under like that!"

"I wasn't drowning myself. I just wanted to be under the water for a while."

"Why?"

I shrugged. "It's nice under there."

He threw his hands up. "It's nice under there. Great. I'm glad. I'm glad that you had a *nice* time enjoying your near-drowning. You're drunk, clumsy, and accident prone as hell. You can't be taking risks with your life like that. You could've gotten caught on something. Then what? What would you have done then, huh?"

I met his angry stare and hiccupped. "P.O.L.A.R. would've gotten a better, more competent replacement."

"Not fucking funny. I'm not fucking laughing right now, Kerrigan. See my face. Serious as shit." He pointed his finger at his chin. "You're a fucking menace to yourself."

13

KERRIGAN

"Ou think I don't know that?" My calm demeanor seemed to throw Dmitry for a loop. I just kept staring at him, accepting that we were going to have whatever conversation he wanted. That's how things seemed to work—everything on his terms.

He paced in front of me, his bare feet leaving a trench in the sand. "What's wrong with you?"

I laughed. "I don't think you have the time."

"Try me." He came to a stop in front of me and stared at me. "Tell me what's going on."

I hiccupped again and pulled my knees into my chest, locking my arms around them. "I owe someone money."

"The guy who's been hanging around you?"

I didn't even need to ask how he known about Nicky Knuckles showing up. The bears seemed to know everything. "Yeah. I borrowed a lot of money from him and I've been paying it back, but he wants more."

"You borrowed money from a loan shark?" He sounded incredulous.

"Yes. Well, no...but, yes."

"Well, which is it?"

"I didn't know that's what he was at the time. Not really. I needed money and I heard his name mentioned around campus a few times. So, I went to him."

"How much did you borrow?"

"Ten thousand."

Dmitry swore and started his pacing again. "Why, Kerrigan? What would possibly make you do that? Ten thousand dollars from a loan shark? Jesus."

"He was my last resort and I just did it."

"What'd you need it for?"

I looked past him, out at the ocean. It was calling me back. "School. I was a year away from finishing my master's. I did everything else. I took out student loans, applied for grants and scholarships, worked two part time jobs. Still, I needed more."

"For school?" It was obvious he thought I was an idiot.

"Yes, for school. I didn't know...anything. I didn't know who he was or how he would be." I shrugged. "But, I've made the payments. I haven't missed a month since I took the loan, but he keeps leaning on me for more."

"And now he's threatening you?"

I met Dmitry's eyes and nodded before looking away. "He wants double."

"Or what?"

"It doesn't matter."

"Or what, Kerrigan?"

"Or the usual. What do men always threaten women with? He's a typical sleazeball and certainly not original." I rested my chin on my knees and sighed. I'd quickly lost pretty much all my buzz. It was probably for the best.

"Fuck."

"It's fine. I'll handle it. I'm just trying to hold him off until I get paid on Friday. I'll sign over my paycheck, and he'll go away for another month."

"You won't have anything to live off of. And that won't put a stop to it. You jump through that hoop and he'll demand triple next month." Dmitry squatted in front of me and met my gaze. "What exactly do you mean by 'the usual'? What is he threatening you with? Be specific and spell it out for me. I have to be sure."

I blinked away sudden tears. "He has girls in Miami, apparently. He wants me to…you know…work off some of my debt by servicing his clients." I didn't know what I was going to do. Drinking had been so temporary it had hardly been worth it. And in the end, even that had landed me right in the arms of Nicky Knuckles.

"You're saying he runs a prostitution ring in Miami and he's threatening to pimp you out if you don't increase the payments?"

I swallowed a lump in my throat and stood up. My life sucked. I scooped up my clothes and turned to walk away.

Dmitry growled and stopped me with a hand on my waist. "You've got bruises."

I looked over my shoulder at what I could see of my lower back. Sure enough, there were bruises from Nicky's fingers. I was so drunk at the time, I hadn't even felt them. "They're not gonna kill me."

I pushed Dmitry's hand away and started towards the house. There was no point in explaining anything else to Dmitry. He just wanted to judge me and point out what a lonely idiot I was.

"Kerrigan, stop."

I kept walking. I still swayed a bit, but I walked with enough determination that I made it to the house and up the first flight of stairs to the front door without a problem.

"He can't do that." Dmitry caught my arm and pulled me to a stop. He didn't let go and when he looked at me, I wondered if he was remembering the same thing I was remembering. He just shook his head and frowned, though. "I will not let him do that."

I looked down at my feet and wondered where I'd left my shoes. "People like him do what they want. Don't worry about it, though. It's not your problem."

"It *is* my problem."

My heart skipped a beat and I looked up at him, a sliver of hope daring to emerge. "Why?"

"You work for P.O.L.A.R." He let go of me and stepped back. "You're part of us. Part of the team."

Right. Part of the team. Hardly. I was the weakest link. In fact, my job with the team was skating on such thin ice I was about to drown in the pond. I sighed and pushed open the door. "Ha! That's a laugh."

Hannah was coming out of the kitchen and spotted me. "Kerrigan! What happened to you?"

I looked down at my underwear and sandy clothes clutched to my stomach. "Um... Nothing. Nothing happened. I'm going to take a shower and then head to bed. It's been a long day."

She looked behind me at Dmitry, and frowned. "I'll walk you up."

"You don't have to do that."

"I want to." She smiled and linked her arm through mine. "That's what friends are for."

14

DMITRY

I watched her climb the stairs on shaky legs and waited until Hannah escorted her into her bedroom before I looked away. My heartrate was finally starting to return to a normal pace after the scare she gave me. Seeing Kerrigan go under and not come back up had convinced me of two things. One, she needed me to protect her. Two, I needed her to be safe.

Fury like I'd never felt ignited within me. Every dark thought and every torture technique I'd ever heard of were begging to be unleashed on the man who was threatening her. My bear didn't need the darkness to help. He was bloodthirsty. He wanted to tear the man apart with his teeth and make it a slow, painful death.

I needed more information. When Kerrigan was sober, I was going to get it all out of her. I needed his name and where he was from. I was going to make it right for her. No matter what I had to do. She couldn't survive the way she was going and I wasn't going to let her go under the water again. Not on my watch.

"What's up? Was everything okay with Kerrigan earlier?" Serge put down his sandwich and looked at me expectantly.

I hesitated. If it did come to me having to eliminate the asshole threatening Kerrigan, the less Serge knew, the better. "Yeah, I just needed her input on something and I couldn't find her. Problem solved."

"Yeah, okay. I completely buy that."

I shrugged. "Buy it or don't. Are there more sandwiches where that one came from?"

He scowled. "Make it yourself. If there's anything I need to know about Kerrigan, I expect you to tell me, Dmitry."

"What could you possibly need to know about Kerrigan?"

"That's what I'm asking you."

Hannah walked back into the kitchen and stepped against her mate's side. "What are you two arguing about?"

Serge fed some of his sandwich to his mate. "Is there anything going on with Kerrigan?"

Hannah smiled. "Is there a woman on this earth that doesn't have something going on?"

"Anything that I need to know? As her boss?"

"Not that I know of. I think she's just torn up about a guy."

Serge groaned. "Never mind. Forget I asked."

My appetite was suddenly ruined. I nodded a goodbye to them and went up to my room. I could hear the shower running and sat on the edge of my bed, waiting for the water to shut off.

It was pure torture. Since I'd held Kerrigan in the very spot I was sitting at that moment, my mind had been going in circles. I'd been beside myself. Seeing her, hearing her voice, thinking about her, all of it was painful.

Knowing she was naked in the next room over was bad enough, but knowing that she was hurting made me ache. I knew why. My bear knew what it was. She was ours and I couldn't stand her pain. She was under my skin bigtime.

When the water cut off, I waited a few minutes and then went across to Kerrigan's room. I lightly knocked on the door and waited for her to answer.

"Hang on." Her voice sounded tired. "Just a sec."

I leaned against the doorframe waiting for her to let me in. After a few seconds, I could sense her hovering by the door, thinking about whether or not she should open it. She was angry and hurt, both of which were justifiable. I needed to be in that room with her, though. "Let me in, Kerrigan."

She sighed and pulled the door open. Blocking me from coming in, she stared down at the floor. "What do you want?"

My bear grumbled low in my chest, but I cut him off. It didn't matter what the fuck he wanted. I needed to make sure Kerrigan was safe. That took priority over everything. "I want to finish talking."

She groaned and shook her head, but I took advantage of my size and leaned into the room and into her personal space until she reflexively stepped aside. Dirty trick, but I needed to be in the room with her. I needed to make sure she was safe.

"You can't just—"

"I can and I am." I walked over to the window, pushed it closed, and latched it. Then, I slid her curtains closed and turned to face her. She'd been hiding herself behind the door, so it was my first full look at her since I'd entered. She took my breath away.

The oversized t-shirt she wore stopped mid-thigh and fell off her right shoulder. Her hair was damp and piled on the top of her head in a loose, spiky bun with a few stray strands hanging in her face. Her eyes looked even larger than normal behind her thick glasses. Her perfectly shaped lips were puckered out in displeasure as she watched me, slim arms crossed over her chest.

I'd just seen her in her underwear, but something about her bare shoulder and bare stretch of leg from toe to thigh was killing me. That exposed shoulder should've been illegal.

I took a deep breath and inhaled her fresh, clean scent. Okay, that didn't help, so I turned back to the window and took a minute to compose myself. "We have to come up with a plan to keep you safe."

Bare feet padded across the floor. The bed let out a light squeak as she sat on it. It was the ruffling of the bedding that caused me to turn around. She was getting under the covers.

"What are you doing?"

"I'm tired. I don't want to talk." She looked over at me and, in a rare moment of steady eye contact, she held my gaze while she pulled the blanket up to her chin. "You should leave. It doesn't look right."

Frowning, I shrugged. "It's fine. We're just talking, Kerrigan."

She popped up like a jack in a box, her face flushing as red as her lips. "It's not fine. It's the farthest thing from fine. After what happened…between us… You haven't said two words to me about that."

I grunted. "I'm sorry."

"Oh, my gosh. Don't apologize! Do you think that's what I want to hear?" She clutched the blanket in a death grip and stared at it. "*That* happened between us and then you kicked me out and apologized. You don't want me? Fine. I'm a big girl. I can accept rejection and I can move past it. What I can't accept is you coming in here and talking to me like it's not weird that we're both this close to my bed and I'm not wearing any underwear."

I guess I had a funny bone somewhere deep inside that I hadn't known existed because I wanted to laugh. Not at her, but just… because. She was cute. More than cute, she was beautiful and intelligent and irritating, and perfect.

"Why are you looking at me like that?"

I straightened my face and shrugged. "Like what?"

"Like you want to laugh at me. Is it funny that I thought you might have actually wanted to be with me? It probably is, isn't it? You're this hot looking hero guy and I'm this mousy little four-eyed virgin. Literally, the last thing on your mind is someone like me. I guess the other day was just scratching an itch with whomever was available? I just happened to be in the right place at the right time? Lucky me. It's terrible to laugh at someone because they have a crush on you." She gasped a big breath and turned a heated stare on me. Her bottom lip began to wobble. "Please go. I'm not drunk anymore, but I still might cry about this."

15

KERRIGAN

"*I*'m not going anywhere." To prove his point, Dmitry pulled out my desk chair and sat in it, his long legs spread out in front of him. "And I'm not laughing at you."

I felt disoriented. I'd worked up a big anger and he'd just deflated my anger balloon. "What?"

"I'm not going anywhere." He crossed his arms over his chest and rolled his neck. "And I'm not laughing at you. Got it?"

I turned to face him and shook my head. "No, I don't 'got it.'"

He watched my finger quotes with another one of those little smirks on his face. "I'm going to make sure you're safe. I don't like the idea of you being in here by yourself, so far away from help."

"Across the hall is far away?"

Ignoring me, he continued. "This way, I can make sure you're safe and no one is trying to sneak in through your window."

My stomach twisted at the idea of Nicky Knuckles climbing in through my bedroom window. I turned and stared at it like it was a four-headed monster with drool on its fangs.

"No one is coming in, Kerrigan. I'm staying right here to make sure of that."

"Why?"

He shifted. "Because."

"That's not an answer."

"It's the only one you're getting."

I kicked the covers off my legs and sat on the edge of the bed. My feet were just inches from his. Oddly, I wanted to rub my feet against his so some part of us touched. I wasn't a martyr, though. I could only take so much rejection.

"Did it feel to you like I didn't care who I was with, Kerrigan?" The husky tone of Dmitry's voice surprised me and when I glanced up at him, it was clear by his expression he was expecting an answer.

I bit my lip and played with the hem of my T-shirt. I was afraid to lay all my cards out in front of him. It was so obvious to me that he had all the power in our exchanges. I needed to keep something close to my vest. "I don't know."

"I'll tell you, then. I knew absolutely who I was with and you were exactly who I wanted. It was how rough I was with you that I am sorry about, but not for touching you or tasting you. That I'm not sorry for."

My stomach fluttered. "Oh."

"It's pretty obvious that the desire was there long before that night."

South of my stomach fluttered, too. I found a worn spot on the hem of my shirt and tugged at a thread. "It wasn't. Pretty obvious, I mean."

As if he realized that he was saying too much, he grew quiet, but I could feel his eyes on me. They burned like a thousand suns over my skin.

I licked my suddenly dry lips and scooted back into bed. "None of it matters, anyway. Even if there was desire, or whatever, I signed a contract. If anyone found out about what happened, I'd lose my job. And, as you know, I can't afford to lose this job."

"What? What contract?"

I made a big deal of fluffing my pillows. "To work here, I had to sign a non-fraternization contract. Dating or otherwise engaging in romantic or sexual relations with team members is grounds for my immediate dismissal."

"You're not serious."

I looked up and found that he'd sat forward, his eyes, more smoky gray than dark blue right then, locked onto me. Nodding, I shrugged. "Yeah, I signed it before coming here. I just figured it was normal. Although, I guess I can see why they didn't make any of you sign it. None of you seem to want to date each other."

He cocked his head to the side.

Realizing what I'd said, I sped ahead, into oncoming word traffic. "I mean, it's fine if you do. I'm not judging or anything. I was talking about us, anyway. *Me*. Not you. I don't want to imply that you wanted to sleep with me. I mean, it's obvious that you don't. Don't feel the need to make that any clearer, okay? Or say anything at all. No comment necessary."

Still, Dmitry said nothing. His eyes were so still and focused on me, his head was cocked slightly to the side as he listened.

"Well, anyway. I should get some sleep."

"It's not even dark out yet."

"And still, somehow, I've managed to tire myself out." I sank back under the covers, needing the protection of a blanket to hide myself.

"Kerrigan..."

I held up my hand to stop him. "I do not want to hear anything you feel you need to say in reply to my verbal diarrhea. In fact, I'd really appreciate if we could both pretend I didn't say any of it. So, I'm going to go to sleep. You should go back to your room. I don't need a babysitter."

Dmitry was nice enough to be silent after that. He stayed where he was, though, which was torture enough. My body was so overtly aware that he was in the room and only a few feet from my bed, that I couldn't think of anything else. All I could do was lie there and squeeze my eyes shut, hoping I'd fall asleep as fast as possible.

Miraculously, having Dmitry that close seemed to also settle a restlessness deeper within me. Under the sexual tension, I realized all of my other fears had faded enough that I wasn't worrying about them. It allowed me to fall asleep and I slept like the dead. The only thing stirring me throughout the night were dreams of Dmitry.

16

DMITRY

$\mathcal{M}$y heartrate didn't return to normal until Kerrigan had been asleep for several hours. I pondered what she'd said—and what she hadn't said. I was all but sitting on my hands to keep them away from her, but no way was I going to touch her. I couldn't. The contract. Her confirmed virginity. I was bad news for her. I just sat as she slept.

I watched over her, with heavy lids tracing her outline, memorizing the details that made up Kerrigan. Her bare shoulder peeked out from under the blanket. Her skin was smooth and looked like silk. Without her thick glasses on, her face was fine-featured. Flat, delicate nose. Fringe of short, dark lashes brushing her cheeks. When she turned, I noticed a dark birthmark on the back of her shoulder that looked like one of the astral constellations. I couldn't remember which one.

My mother had been into the stars. She would give readings and map astrological charts for clients, telling all sorts of stories based on the position of the stars. It'd been so long since she'd passed. I couldn't remember any astrology. That whimsical kind of thing had never mattered to me when I was young. The stars, the moon and sun, all of them were just...out there. I do remember one particular story, though. I remember her talking about how the stars had aligned just right for her and my father, and that the same would happen for me one day.

What would my mother think of me now? Seeing that constellation shaped birthmark on Kerrigan's shoulder touched me deeply. I wished my mother could have met Kerrigan. For the first time in quite a while, in the darkness of the room, I found myself mourning the loss of my mother.

With the sorrow of loss came a mighty dose of reality. Life was fragile. Even a shifter's life. Things happened. People died. Everything about Kerrigan was fragile, small and virtually defenseless.

I knew she was my mate. I'd known it the moment I'd first set eyes on her. She'd walked into the P.O.L.A.R. office with Serge and my jaw had dropped clear to the floor. When her eyes drifted to mine, even hidden behind thick glasses, I thought I saw recognition in them as well. She'd looked away quickly, but not before I noticed the way her cheeks had flushed.

How the stars could have aligned to send me someone as pure and delicate and perfect as Kerrigan, I would never know. I was undoubtedly damned, my soul as dark as the deepest depths of the ocean. My story was set, my deeds committed. Nothing I could ever do would make up for the acts I'd already wrought. Why fate would give me Kerrigan was a mystery. I wasn't right for her. Christ, my fantasies alone, the things I wanted to do to her were dirtier than a woman like her ever deserved.

None of it made sense to me, but I'd at least accepted the truth. We were mates, but we needed to refrain from consummating the mating or going through with the claiming.

Even if it weren't for the fact that I didn't deserve her, the contract she'd signed would've made things too difficult for her. The main office would fire her, without a doubt. If they'd gone as far as to make her sign something so fucking asinine, they would surely stand by it.

I didn't want to cost her the job she needed, although I would handle her debt myself, and I should've been grateful for the excuse to stay away from her. I didn't feel grateful. I felt pissed off that the company I worked for would dare to think they could dictate something so personal to Kerrigan. They had no right to control what she did on her own time and with whom.

I knew it was a direct response to Serge and Hannah mating while he was on the job. It had led to the team breaking protocol and disobeying direct orders. The contract was their way of showing us that we didn't get to pull a stunt like that again. Actually, the more I thought about it, the more it pissed me off. If Kerrigan did "fraternize" with one of us, she would lose her job and we would, what? Get a slap on the wrist? A high five? Way to go, bro? Men will be men and all that? Fuck that.

As soon as I handled things with Kerrigan's loan shark, I was going to have plenty to say to the main office. They'd get an earful from me. I was already ticked that they'd jerked the team around by sending us here from Siberia. They'd punished us and were continuing to do so by keeping us on the island, where we weren't doing any real work. To think they could keep our mates away from us, if and when we found them, was overreaching.

We were trained operatives but, especially when it came to mates, we were shifters, too. Looking at Kerrigan's sleeping form, I felt like a man first, operative second, shifter third. Maybe that's what the main office was trying to stop from happening—an operative valuing a mate over the job.

I knew that I would fight twice as hard as I'd ever fought if I was fighting to keep her safe. Just like Serge and Roman with their mates.

Kerrigan rolled over and softly spoke my name in her sleep. She did that almost every night. Maybe I was an asshole for keeping my ears peeled and prying into her private moments, but I didn't know how to stop.

I stood up and paced over to the window, pulling just the edge of the curtain back so I could stare out into the night. Nothing but the expanse of ocean and sky stared back at me.

Her loan shark wasn't coming for her, yet. But when he did, he wasn't going to like what he found. Twice, he'd gotten to her. He'd left bruises on her body. Never again. He was either going to go away peacefully, or he was going to wish he'd never set eyes on Kerrigan Tran. I'd make sure of that.

17

KERRIGAN

*W*hat had I been thinking getting wasted on a Monday night? I felt like a Mack truck had run over my head and my stomach wasn't much better. Worse than either was my pride. That was so wounded that I couldn't meet anyone's eyes at work the next morning. I felt like everyone knew all of my dirty secrets. I *knew* Dmitry knew them.

I was horrified at how I'd behaved in front of him. Flashbacks of the verbal onslaught alone were enough to send me scrambling for the bathroom that morning in a wave of nausea. At least in the bathroom I could avoid having to look at him or see him laughing. Even if he said he hadn't been laughing at me, I didn't believe him. How could he not? I'd made a complete ass of myself.

My head throbbed and my stomach cramped. I sat at my desk with my head down and tried to pretend like I was a braver woman, someone who would've seduced Dmitry into her bed instead of awkwardly flapping my gums and revealing way too much.

Dmitry seemed fine, though. He brought me a cup of coffee, with one sugar the way I liked it, and handed me a small bottle of Tylenol. He turned the air conditioners down, too. Their normal humming had been lowered to something tolerable, despite the rest of the team grumbling and giving him shit about how hot it was. He was hot, too. When I dared look up, I could see the sweat bloom on the back of his shirt. Still, he kept the AC down.

I didn't know why he was being nice. Why hadn't he gone running for the hills after last night.

The guys were all in the office, suffocating me. They were loud and, no matter where I needed to go, in my way. Getting them to move was always a project. I just wanted the office to myself for the morning to be able to readjust, but it was impossible.

When the phone rang, I was so eager for them to leave, that I answered it faster than I ever had before. As I listened, I hastily repeated what I heard, calling out the address and code to the men, ready for them to leave and give me a break.

"998?" Serge hesitated and gave me a stern look. "Are you sure?"

I nodded. "That's what they said."

After the guys came out a few minutes later with a huge cage and a gun bigger than me, I started to second guess myself. My stomach somersaulted and I pressed my hand to it. The person on the phone had said 998, I was pretty sure. That was a big gun, though.

"You're sure?" Serge had a protective mask in his hand and kept giving me that hard stare.

It was too late to take it back. I nodded and looked down at my paperwork, wanting the interaction to be over.

Dmitry stopped next to my desk and tapped his finger on it twice. "Lock the door behind us, Kerrigan."

My heart fluttered, the stupid thing, and I nodded awkwardly. "Okay."

I did like he said and locked the door. I hoped I hadn't just told them to go somewhere dangerous, but most of all I hoped I hadn't gotten the message wrong. I didn't think Serge was going to give me another chance. He didn't even like me.

To add to my headache and heartache, my mom called right when I sat back down at my desk. While I would've normally screened her call, she called on the office line and I didn't know it was her until too late.

"Mom, this is an emergency line."

"I won't talk long. I just wanted to see how things were going." Her voice seemed far away.

I squeezed my eyes shut and dug my nails into my palm to keep from crying. I was a grown woman. I had no business crying to my mom. "Things are fine."

"I heard you're having some trouble adjusting." She hesitated. "If they let you go, I don't have anything else, honey."

I bit my lip and made a sound of acknowledgement.

"Just try your hardest." Laughter sounded in the background and her voice lifted in joy. "Sorry, Kerrigan, I have to let you go. We're on the ski slopes. Just do your best, honey."

I put the phone back down in its cradle and blew out a big breath. Talks with my mom always went like that. Disappointment with me and eagerness get off the line. It had been that way since she'd met her mate when I was in my second year of college. I was a problem and the rest of her life was amazing.

I took another Tylenol and swallowed it with cold coffee. I was just getting up to file more paperwork when the locked front door burst open, both the lock and the doorknob flying across the room. I screamed and shielded my face with the files in my hand.

"Kerrigan! How fucking hard is it to listen to a phone message and repeat it?!" Serge was suddenly in front of me, his face bright red, a vein in his forehead pulsing. "Do you have any idea what you just had us do?"

Cringing away from him, I prayed for the floor to open up and swallow me whole.

"You sent us on a run to capture a rabid shifter. At the home of a nice young *human* computer programmer." He seethed. "We had him in the cage wetting himself before realizing we'd just tranquilized a human!"

I covered my mouth with my hand and backed away from him. "I didn't mean…"

"I should fire your ass right now. I should send you back to your car and let you go on to ruin someone else's business."

I was going to cry. I tried hard to fight it, but—his shouting...and my horror. I'd messed up again.

"We're stuck in this sweatbox because of fuckups. With you working here, we're never going to get our asses back home. Tell me why I shouldn't fucking fire you on the spot!"

I didn't have a reason that wasn't purely self-motivated. I stuttered out an apology, but I was choking on tears and I couldn't get it out very clearly. It just seemed to make Serge angrier.

"Cry all you want. It doesn't make me any less furious with you."

I wiped at my eyes and hurried over to my desk. Time to go. He was so angry that there was no way I wasn't fired. What the hell was I still standing there for? I'd just scram and save him the trouble.

"Where are you going?"

I hurried for the door, but Dmitry stepped into my way, his eyes on Serge behind me. I watched as a fine layer of white fur rippled across his face and his eyes glowed. He reached out and pulled me towards him and then behind him. "Wait outside."

18

DMITRY

*K*errigan didn't need to see what was about to happen. Moving farther into the office, I growled low in my throat at Serge. I didn't give a fuck who he was, Alpha or not, he wasn't going to treat my mate like that.

"Don't start with me right now, Dmitry."

I curled my lip and bared my teeth, showing him how serious I was. "You want to scream at someone, scream at me. Pick on someone your own size."

"Fuck off. I'm not picking on her. You were there. You know how bad that was. You really want to let that shit happen again?"

"You don't scream at her." I rolled my neck from side to side and sneered at him. "You scream at Hannah like that?"

That did the trick. Serge was instantly as ready to brawl as I was. "Don't fucking bring my mate into this."

"You started it." I took advantage of his shock. Charging at him, I slammed into his stomach with my shoulder and sent us flying backwards.

The fight was on. I forgot that Serge was my boss and a friend. I was strung out so tightly and so angry that I just needed to brawl. Serge was pissed, too, though, and he gave just as good as he got.

Desks and chairs that were innocently caught in our path were flattened, the front door was left hanging off of its hinges, file cabinets were upended. We beat the shit out of each other.

Serge shifted and pinned me down with one giant paw on my chest. Growling in my face, drool dripping from his canines, he let out a mighty roar that shook the walls of the office.

It did the job of breaking through haze of fury I'd been in. I blinked a few times and looked up at him, instantly regretting that I'd gone after him so hard. I let my head hit the floor under me and groaned.

He shifted back and landed one last painful punch to my ribs—a cheap shot. "I'm fucking sick of you assholes fighting me."

I grunted and sat up. "You deserved this one."

He stared at me hard for a full minute before shaking his head. "Maybe you're right. I shouldn't have yelled at her."

My fists balled up at my sides. "Don't ever do it again."

He grunted that time. "She can't keep working here if it keeps happening."

I shrugged. "We'll see."

"I'm serious, Dmitry. We look like clowns. No way are we ever going to get back to Siberia like this. They're going to send us to the fucking Sahara at this rate."

I looked over my shoulder and tried to spot Kerrigan. "I'll help her."

"Do something." He stood up and offered me a hand. When I tried to take it, he let go and watched me fall back. "Don't fucking pull that shit again. Tell her I'm sorry."

"Tell her your fucking self." I climbed to my feet and went out to find her and see that she was okay.

Alexei grinned at me when he saw me. "Nice one. You really picked a fight with Serge, huh?"

I ignored him. "Where's Kerrigan?"

Konstantin looked up from studying his shoes. "She headed toward the house. She looked pretty freaked out."

Fuck. I'd scared her. I hurried towards the house, needing to see

72

her and convince her that everything was okay, despite also wondering if it wasn't better to just let her continue to think I was a monster. I couldn't, though. The idea of her scared of me was intolerable.

I heard her crying as soon as I entered the house. Not that she was crying loudly, but I was tuned into her. She was in her room sitting on her bed, her face buried in her hands. Her door was ajar, just a hair, so I pushed it open, stepped in, and squatted in front of her.

"I'm sorry, Kerrigan."

She jerked upright and turned away from me. Sniffing and wiping at her face, she cleared her throat. "Um, I'm just... I'm fine."

I sat on the bed next to her, but she was turned so her back was to me. Close enough to touch, I still didn't. "I didn't mean to scare you."

She swayed, her back coming closer to me. "You didn't."

I inched closer. "It's okay if you were freaked out, Kerrigan. I shouldn't have shown my anger in front of you like that. I should've remained calm and just talked to Serge about the way he treated you."

Her neck was bare, her hair pulled up. I could see the tail end of that constellation shaped birthmark. "*He* scared me. You didn't. But, I didn't like that you were fighting for me. You... You shouldn't have to fight for me."

Giving in, I closed the gap, pressing my stomach against her back, feeling her shiver against me. Still, I kept my hands to myself. "I want to fight for you."

She let out a little sigh, more exhale than anything. "I deserved his anger. I do suck at the job. I keep messing up. If I wasn't so hard up for money, I'd quit so he could hire someone worthwhile."

"You are worthwhile." I slowly lifted my hands and hovered just above her shoulders. My heart thudded in my chest and I barely stifled a possessive growl. "You're more than worthwhile."

She pressed herself back into my chest. "I don't know what's going to happen now."

I dropped my hands back to my side. "Nothing's going to happen. Everything's fine. Serge shouldn't have yelled at you. He's sorry. You'll get better at the job."

I heard her sniffle again as she scooted forward a few inches, away from me. She'd sensed my mood change that fast. It was like we were already bonded. Her arms crossed over her chest and she glanced over her shoulder at me with a fake smile. "I'm fine, Dmitry. Go back to work."

I didn't want to leave her. I could hear the pain in her voice. She was not fine. She deserved better.

Backing out of the room, I pulled her door closed and stood there for a moment, wrestling with the urge to go back in. It was painful to walk away, but it was for the best.

KERRIGAN

I turned to watch the door close and let out the breath I'd been holding. I bit my fingernail and stared, like I was going to be able to see him through the door. I didn't know what was happening, but what I did know was that Dmitry had fought for me. The feeling of his body pressed against mine was seared onto my skin. The way he'd stared at me, his eyes so intense, all signs that he was interested in me. Yet, he withdrew every time.

My emotions were all over the place. I was getting neurotic about Dmitry and whether he wanted me or not. My entire mood seemed to depend on how interactions between us played out. I'd never been that way. I'd never been all that concerned with how men felt about me. Dmitry was the first—in so many ways. My feelings for him were different—deeper. I couldn't break through his walls, though. He kept me at an arm's length. Which, now that I thought about it, was probably was a pretty solid sign.

I grabbed my notebook; I needed to write. The feelings he inspired —his chest pressed against my back—bounced around my brain until it was all I could think about. I let myself have time to get everything out on paper and then changed into a nice sundress and sandals.

Getting my thoughts out on paper was often an exercise in

clearing my mind, gaining greater insight, and a perhaps developing a new perspective. And, in this instance, it had worked. Another idea began to solidify in my brain. I had to find another job. Not only was working at P.O.L.A.R. killing what little confidence I had, but I couldn't figure out what was going on with Dmitry until I had a job to fall back on. If I didn't have to depend on P.O.L.A.R., I could, as Grandma, may she rest in peace, would have said, shit or get off the pot.

I hadn't had any luck before Mom helped me get the dispatcher job, but now that I'd relocated to Sunkissed Key, maybe there was something on the island. I could at least try. I'd go back to living in my car until I could afford a place of my own.

I made my way out of the house and to Main Street on a mission. I headed north, away from P.O.L.A.R., and looked in at all the different businesses. I put in applications at Clotilde's Creamery, a lovely old fashioned ice cream shop, Latte Love, the coffee shop, as well as the grocery store. I stopped in at Rise and Shine Bed and Breakfast. They weren't hiring, but a purple haired woman with tattoos asked me to sign her petition—something about endangered rabbits on the island.

I tried Mimi's Cabana, and another bar called Cap'n Jim's. No go. It wasn't looking good. At the far end of the island was Sunkissed Key Wildlife Sanctuary, not hiring.

After exhausting all my options on Main Street, I tried side streets. They were mostly lined with residential homes, but at the very end of Parrot Cove Road, off of West Public Beach, I found the Bayfront Diner. I figured it was worth a shot. Plus, I was getting hungry. I ordered a cinnamon roll and sweet tea and spoke with the owner, a sweet woman named Susie.

Susie was older, with a beehive of steel-gray hair, and reminded me of Alice from the Brady Bunch. Her full figure was covered in a bright blue apron, and her smile was as warm as the Florida sunshine.

Her eyes had lit up when I told her I was job hunting. She'd made me fill out an application and then told me that I needed sunscreen if I was going to be walking up and down the island.

After leaving Susie's, I hit a lull. I didn't want to apply anywhere else. I wanted to work for her. She was like happiness in a bottle, pouring little bits out with every stroke of her pen on her order pad. I meandered around the island for a bit more, remaining alert, quite aware that Nicky Knuckles was possibly still around and could pop out from a dark alley or from around a corner at any moment.

I ended up at the beach on the east side of the island, hoping to avoid any and all of the team members. I sat in the sand and watched the ocean gently lap the shore. Wrapping my arms around myself, I stayed there as the sun moved across the sky, determined to pretend I didn't exist for a while. I felt the sun heat my skin and remembered what Susie had warned about using sunscreen, but I didn't want to move.

"Kerrigan?"

I jumped, shocked out of my trance. Looking over my shoulder, I was shocked to see Megan. "Hey. What are you doing here?"

She pointed to the house behind me. "I live there."

I suddenly felt as though I was intruding on her space, and quickly got to my feet dusting sand off. "Oh, I really had no idea. I just ended up on this side of the island and decided to sit on the beach and watch the water."

She smiled and nodded behind her to her house. "Come on inside. I need to put these groceries down."

I started to shake my head, but she looked hopeful and I didn't want to offend her by refusing. "Sure."

She led the way, talking to me over her shoulder. "How have you been? I've been meaning to organize another get together with you and Hannah, but I've been busy trying to remodel this porch. I decided that I wanted a little something extra special, but it's turned into a pain in the ass."

"You're doing it yourself?"

She pushed open the door and led me into a beautifully decorated home. Amongst the decor were tools of all sizes, discarded clothes, and a few boxes of take out. "Ignore the mess. Roman and I have been kind of...busy."

I trailed behind her into the kitchen, knowing perfectly well what she meant by *busy*. She and Roman were newly mated. I forced out thoughts of Dmitry that tried to surface. "Your house is beautiful."

"Yeah, well. I lost some things when my ex left. It's going to take me time to get everything back to the way it's supposed to be." She started putting groceries away and sighed. "Life, you know?"

Perched on the edge of a stool, I wrung my hands together and let out a slow exhale. "Um, yeah."

Megan paused with her hand halfway up to a cabinet, a jar of sauce frozen in the air. "What's wrong, Kerrigan? You look shaken."

I ran my hands down my dress and fought with a brittle smile. "I'm okay."

"No, I don't believe that. Come on. The rest of these groceries can wait. Let's sit on my couch and talk. You look like you need some girl talk."

"No, really. I'm okay. It's just been a long day."

"I'm not taking no for an answer. And I have wine." She waggled her eyebrows. "Just talk to me about today. Nothing else, if you don't want to."

I studied her for a second, everything about her seemed together and as though her life was in order. I turned and looked out of the window. "How do you keep everything in your life so together? How does everyone around me have their shit so together? We're around the same age. Why am I so far behind everyone else?"

She frowned. "Behind everyone else? What do you mean?"

"My mom got me my job. I suck at it and I'm one minor screw up away from being fired. I lived in my car until Serge insisted I move into the house with the team. I'm still a virgin and lusting after a man who doesn't seem to be very interested in me most of the time. I have no pets. I cry all the time. My credit score is crap. Literally, I feel like I'm a failure at adulting." I turned back to face her and blinked faster in an attempt to keep the tears at bay. "I spent so much time in school, working hard to earn a degree in English and creative writing, but for what? I write all the time but I can't get a novel published. I have so many loans and nothing to really show for them. I put my life on hold to get through school and pay for it myself and now, I'm trying to live and I have no clue what I'm doing."

Megan scooted closer to me and gently wrapped her arm around my shoulder. "Oh, sweetie. None of us know what we're doing. And it's not a race."

I sank into her side and wiped at my eyes. "I'm sorry. I didn't mean to cry on you. I just… I'm feeling so lost."

She hugged me harder and rested her head against mine. "It's okay. We're friends, right?"

I laughed. "Are we? You might want to rethink that. I'm not kidding you when I say that I'm a mess."

"Well, dry your eyes, sunshine. You and I are friends. Hannah, too. And this is what friends are for. To hug you and comfort you, but also to tell you to stop being so hard on yourself. You're not doing any worse than any of the rest of us. I just watched my entire life crumble to dust and had to restart from scratch. Hannah had her life upended and relocated here because of being mated to Serge. None of us really have it that together. We're all just trying to do the best we can."

I blew out breath and smiled shakily. "I'm glad you and Hannah are my friends. I could really use a couple of friends right now."

20

DMITRY

*A*fter leaving Kerrigan's room, I went back to work and tapped into all the techniques in my arsenal trying to remain calm and levelheaded. By the end of the workday, I was so tense I felt like I was going to snap in half at any moment. I hurried back to the house feeling lighter from knowing I'd find Kerrigan inside. But, she wasn't there.

My bear demanded to be let out so he could comb the island until he found her, but I had a different agenda. *I'm looking for someone.*

I sent out all of the details I knew about Kerrigan's loan shark and searched the beach while waiting to see if the rest of the guys found anything. If Kerrigan needed space, I wouldn't intrude. But, I needed to make sure she was safe and her absence had nothing to do with a certain slimy loan shark.

Not even ten minutes later, Maxim came through. *At Mimi's now. I think your man is here.*

Make sure he doesn't leave. I raced across Main Street and through a neighborhood to get to Mimi's, eager to nab that asshole. The fucker had to go.

Sure enough, the sleazeball was sitting at the bar, smiling at one of

Mimi's female bartenders when I walked in. Maxim was at the back of the bar and tipped his head to me when I walked in.

I went straight to the little weasel and sat down on the stool next to him. When the bartender approached me, I shook my head. She must have read my expression because she backed off with hands raised. "You and I have a problem."

The man put his beer down and turned to me with a nasty scowl on his face. "You talking to me?"

I held his gaze and took a deep breath in an attempt to calm myself and rein my bear in. "Yeah, I am."

He smiled, more a sneer than a smile. "Let's hear it. Why do we have a problem?"

I pulled out my phone and pulled up the app I used to move money. "Kerrigan Tran. You're not going to bother her anymore."

"Oh, that's where I've seen you. You're the sorry sonofabitch who's been trailing along behind her like a lost puppy." He chuckled. "I get it. She's got a nerdy librarian thing going on. You wanna tap that ass, huh?" He leaned forward and lowered his voice. "I could arrange it for a small finder's fee."

I growled and counted to ten. Slowly. "I'm going to pay you what she owes you. Then, you're going to get the fuck off of this island and never return."

His eyes widened. "You're going to pay me?"

"Yeah, I am. Then, you're done with her." I held out my phone for him to enter his information to complete the transfer. "Ten thousand. On top of what she's already paid you."

"Oh, my man. No can do. She owes more than that in interest."

I inched closer to him. "Let me tell you something. You're going to take the money and get the fuck out of here. It's a very generous offer; take my word on that. I'm inches from snapping and you're not going to like what happens if I do. Take the money and go. That's your one and only option."

"There's always a second option."

I bared my teeth. "You're right. The second option includes your remains and a body bag."

Finally, he stopped seeing the humor in the situation. "You asshole."

I shrugged and slid the phone under his nose. "Take the more-than-generous offer. Door number two means having your flesh shredded to ribbons by razor sharp claws longer than your fingers. Let me be clear what that will be like. It will take a few seconds for your brain to process what happened. You'll feel everything. You'll watch yourself fall apart."

He yanked the phone away from me and jabbed at the screen. Finally, he gave it back to me. "I need a couple thousand more for traveling expenses. I had to come all the way out here to the Keys to collect."

"Maybe you didn't hear me. Not a penny more. You chose to fuck with the wrong woman."

Nicholas Palermo, I learned from the info on my phone, stood up and scowled at me. "Fuck you and that bitch."

I stood up, fighting down my anger. Fortunately for him, he was already scurrying for the door. I sat back down and rested my fists on the bar top. It wasn't easy to let him leave, but I didn't just kill in anger. It was always for a reason. He was leaving, holding up his end of the deal, which meant he was safe.

Maxim slid onto the stool beside me and gave a low whistle. "That sounded interesting."

"Asshole has been threatening Kerrigan."

He raised a brow. "You're fighting for her a lot lately."

"She's a nice girl."

He laughed. "Girl? Are we talking about the same Kerrigan? Kerrigan is shy at times, maybe a bit inexperienced, but she's no girl. She's definitely a grown woman. You might want to remember that."

Cutting my eyes to him, I shook my head. "Be careful what you say right now, brother. I'm holding on by a thread."

He held his hands up in front of him. "She's all yours. I was just giving advice. Me? I've got my eye on that sweet little blonde over in the corner, Sheila...or Shelly. Maybe Sharon." He stood up and slapped me on the shoulder. "Shannon. Yeah, it's Shannon. I think."

I looked down at my phone and completed the transaction to Nicholas Palermo, ready to be over and done with him. He'd receive the money, untraceable, and he'd leave Kerrigan alone. If he wanted to live. She'd have one less thing to worry about and I wouldn't have to be afraid of her getting hurt.

"Your friend left you with his bill, Dmitry." Mimi nodded at the door, letting me know she meant sleezeball. "Nice guy, huh?"

I pulled out a couple of bills and dropped them on the bar. "That cover it?"

She nodded. "More than. Is he going to be around a lot?"

I shook my head. "Matter of fact, if he shows up again, call us."

She nodded, handing the money to her bartender, and grinned. "I saw you with my favorite Asian yesterday. She's a sweetie pie, isn't she?"

Standing, I slipped my phone and wallet back into my pocket and held her gaze. "Keep an eye on her if she comes back in. For me."

Mimi laughed. "You men and your demands. Like I told Serge, if you want someone to keep an eye on your ladies, I suggest you do it yourselves. I'm here to help them have a good time."

I growled, frustrated, and headed out. With Nicky taken care of, I wanted to get a handle on where Kerrigan was. Just to check up on her.

21

KERRIGAN

I fell asleep on Megan's couch and woke up to find that it was morning and I'd slept the entire night through. There was a blanket over me and a cup of steaming coffee on the table next to me. I sat up and rubbed at my eyes, feeling sluggish.

"Good morning! I made coffee."

I looked over to see Megan aiming a camera at me. She snapped a photo and then grinned. I winced and ran my hands over my hair. "Sorry I fell asleep."

"No, it's fine. I would have woken you but I figured you needed the sleep. Living in the P.O.L.A.R. house with all that testosterone—and fur—can't be very restful." She made a face. "And I hear that Maxim has a revolving door of female guests."

I shrugged. "I guess I haven't been there long enough to notice."

"Lucky you. Now, smile. These photos are going to be amazing. You're very photogenic." She aimed the camera at me again and snapped a few pictures. "Drink your coffee, too."

I took a huge gulp, managing to burn my tongue, and caught a glimpse of the clock behind her. "Oh, crap. I have to go."

"Wait! One more!" She moved around, the camera still clicking.

"I'm working on a new project and I think these are going to be perfect."

I shoved my feet into my shoes and hurried towards her door. "Thank you for last night, Megan."

"That's what friends are for. Don't forget, drinks tonight!"

I stopped for a second and wrapped her in a hug. "Bye, friend."

I quickly left Megan's and headed toward the P.O.L.A.R. house. I walked across the beach, to Shipwreck Way, and then cut through someone's yard to get to Main Street. Avoiding the office, I went straight to the house, up to my room, and stripped quickly wrapping a towel around my body for the traipse to the shower.

I didn't have time to clean the shower before using it, so I tried not to let my imagination get hung up on what might have gone on in there. I scrubbed up as fast as I could and then hurriedly wrapped the towel back around myself. My glasses were steamed up, but I couldn't see without them and when I opened the door to dart across the hall, still dripping wet...I almost ran smack into Alexei.

As it was, I just bumped him lightly and clutched my towel tighter. "Sorry."

He just smiled. "You okay?"

I met his eyes and nodded. "Just late for work. What are you still doing here?"

"I had a late night. I don't function at my prime with less than nine hours of sleep."

I giggled. "Cause you're a bear."

A loud growl came from the bottom of the stairs and we both looked down to see Dmitry wearing an angry scowl. Alexei held up his hands and scooted around me to get into the bathroom.

I scurried across the hall and was about to close my door when Dmitry caught it and stepped in after me. I gaped at him. "What are you doing, Dmitry?"

"You didn't come home last night."

"I spent the night at Megan's."

"I was worried."

"Why?"

"Because!" He faltered. "Because...someone was threatening you."

I sighed and walked over to my closet. I picked out clothes, aware of his eyes on my back, and tried to remember that I was okay and his opinion of me didn't matter.

"Where'd you go yesterday? Before Megan's?"

Turning to face him, I held his stare and frowned. "I was applying for jobs. Is that okay?"

He took a step back. "What? Why?"

"You know why." I puffed my cheeks and released the air slowly. "I don't want to work for P.O.L.A.R." I didn't need to add that I sucked at the job and Serge was a hair away from firing me anyway. I especially didn't add that I wanted to find another job so I could get up the nerve to demand that Dmitry and I finally engage in the "fraternizing convo". All of the questions and the demanding way he spoke to me, it wasn't normal behavior. I couldn't tell if he liked me or he just felt protective of me—as though I was incapable of taking care of myself.

He turned away from me and gripped the edge of my dresser. "You want to leave?"

I clutched my towel tighter very aware that it was the only thing keeping me for baring it all to him. "Yeah, I do. I want a job that I'm capable at, where I'm not hated."

"No one hates you." He stared at me with intense eyes. "What makes you think that?"

"Well, I don't want to keep walking on eggshells afraid I'm going to screw up and at any second be fired on the spot—lose both my home and my job."

I grabbed my clothes and held them to my chest. "I think we both know that this isn't the job for me. Why do you care anyway? If it's because you think I'm the trouble-bound, worrisome team member, then this works best for both of us. You won't have to worry anymore."

He just shook his head and left, slamming my door behind him.

I huffed out a breath, angry that he hadn't picked up on what I was throwing down. I'd given him a chance to tell me that he didn't want me to go, but he'd just left. I supposed I should take that as an answer.

I got dressed and walked to the office, kicking sand and muttering to myself the whole way.

I didn't even look at Serge when I walked in and sat at my desk. I was mad at him, too. I was mad at everyone. At least I didn't feel like crying, though.

When the phone rang, I was too angry to be nervous. Instead of the main office, however, it was Susie. She invited me to the diner for lunch to discuss the job. I'd had to force myself to not scream with joy. That meant she was considering me—maybe she'd even offer me the job. I might be getting away from P.O.L.A.R. Hopefully.

I hung up and realized that all the men in the room were staring at me. Of course, as shifters, they'd heard the entire conversation. I felt a twinge of shame, but I met Serge's questioning gaze head on and raised my eyebrows. I wanted to crumble under his stare, but I didn't allow myself to.

He just nodded. "Good for you."

I let out a breath I hadn't known I was holding and smiled. Maybe I'd manage to get my life together after all.

22

DMITRY

Kerrigan must have finally realized that I wasn't any good for her. She'd left. After a job interview with Susie at the Bayfront Diner, she packed her things and took off the same night.

I'd thoroughly vetted Susie. The woman had grown up on the island, and her husband Sammy, now deceased, had been from Pensacola. They'd met when he'd vacationed on the island over forty years ago. According to the locals, Sam had dreamed of opening a diner on the west coast, but Susie hadn't wanted to leave Sunkissed Key. They'd compromised and opened their place on the Gulf of Mexico, but named it after the San Francisco Bay.

I was glad that Kerrigan was still on the island, but I could take a hint. She didn't want to be around any of us.

Two days had passed since I'd last seen her hauling her bags down the stairs on Wednesday night. She hadn't asked for help, she hadn't said goodbye, she'd just left.

Kerrigan had probably felt the connection between us, but wanted nothing to do with it. I understood. I had nothing to offer her that she needed. She knew that. I had no idea how to be kind or nurturing or caring. She was sweet, light, gentle. I was dark, ominous, dangerous.

And not fun to be around. I was a speedbump on her road to bigger and better things.

It wasn't hard to imagine her meeting and marrying a nice, regular guy, settling down and having a couple of kids. They'd have a quiet life—family movie nights, a dog or a cat or both, barbecues in the backyard, and the zoo on weekends. Yeah, they'd get to the zoo and look at animals like me in their cages. Maybe take pictures. She'd be happy. She'd be safe.

I had no excuse to complain about any of it. I'd tried to keep Kerrigan at arm's length, and when I had let her closer, I'd been rough and mean. She was smart to run away from me.

Still. I hurt.

I kept reminding myself of why I was no good for Kerrigan. Why I had to stay away. I visited every ghost from my past—every kill, every assassination. I thought about the questionable acts I'd committed. I saw every drop of blood that I'd ever spilled.

My bear mourned her. When he wasn't moping, he was fighting to make me go after her. When I refused, he went into mourning again. It was a vicious cycle.

Work sucked. I finally understood what Roman had gone through when he thought he had lost Megan. He'd been careless. He'd almost been responsible for a roof caving in on his head, and he hadn't much cared. I understood that now.

What was the point? Of *anything* anymore.

"Brother, you look like someone kicked your dog." Alexei strolled into the kitchen, his hair tousled all around his head from the wind outside.

"I don't have a dog."

He stopped. "Okay. What's going on?"

I shook my head and pushed my dinner plate away from me. "Nothing."

He cupped his hand behind his ear as though he was hard of hearing and trying to capture sound. "What's that? Kerrigan, you say? You're fucked up because she left?" He smirked at my shocked look. "Everyone knows, man. Duh. You've been drooling over her since she got here. You attacked Serge because he raised his voice to her. What none of us can understand is why you haven't gone after her."

I scowled. "You think you know so much. You have no idea."

"Is she your mate?"

I opened my mouth and then snapped it shut. Saying it out loud would make it too real, too painful, but I couldn't deny it. I wouldn't deny it. "Yes."

"Then why the fuck are you hanging around here? Go, get her." He rolled his eyes. "You dumb fucks and your mates. You make everything so much harder than it has to be. It's literally as simple as one plus one equals two. You're her mate. She's your mate. Bam."

"It's more complicated than that, smartass."

"Why?"

I stammered. "It just is."

He shook his head. "Or you're making it more complicated. But, hey, if you want a great big mess, fine. I would say it's just on you, but it's not. It's on Kerrigan, too. If you think she's not suffering just as much as you are, you're wrong. She's been waiting on you to make a move since the moment she saw you."

"Shut the fuck up, Alexei. I'm not in the mood."

He held up his hands and backed away. "Okay, okay, I can take a hint. None of my business anyway."

I swore and stood up. "*She* left."

"Yeah, because she was miserable here. Anyone with eyes could've seen that. She didn't like the job and she didn't like being told constantly how she'd fucked things up. She probably also didn't like how the man she was into semi-hooked up with her and then kicked her out of his room."

I snarled. "How do you know that?"

"These walls are paper thin, bro. And you're a fucking idiot."

Anger surged and I wanted to smash his face in. "I have my reasons."

"I'd love to hear them. Matter of fact, I'm sure Kerrigan would love to hear them, too."

"You of all people know what I do, Alexei. Who I am. My unique contribution to this league." I walked to the window and looked out at the ocean. Without even realizing it, my eyes scanned the beach for Kerrigan.

"Save lives?" He came up behind me and rested his hand on my shoulder. "What you do is for a reason, brother. You save more lives than any of us with your 'unique contribution' as you call it. Not a one of us are without blood on our hands, but we do what we do for the common good."

Shaking my head, I stepped away from him. "Do you really believe that?"

He laughed easily, drawing my eyes back to him. "Yes, I do. How do you think I remain so carefree? What we do isn't always pretty, but our job is to save lives and protect the innocent. That's what we do. If there are necessary evils along that path, then so be it. Some of us have to do the dirty work so others can live in peace and freedom. It doesn't change anything, though, Dmitry. You're a good man. And, although I have my occasional doubts about Maxim, the rest of the team is good, too."

"You're serious?"

He nodded. "As a heart attack. So, do whatever you need to do to get over this shit, brother, because you have a mate waiting on you."

I couldn't believe as easily as he did that I was a good man. Even if I was, did I deserve Kerrigan? I didn't think so.

"You think you're doing her a favor, but you didn't see her face when she walked out of here. She's in pain."

I turned away from him again and continued watching the ocean, thinking.

"Don't fuck up."

23

KERRIGAN

"*A*ny plans for the night, pumpkin?" Susie grinned at me, knowing I found her new nickname for me charmingly ridiculous.

"Not much. I have to meet someone to pay a bill. I'm quite the wild weekend partier, you know." I frowned, thinking about it. Nicky Knuckles was the last person I wanted to see, but I had to. He'd been oddly silent, yet when I'd texted him earlier, he'd agreed to meet me.

"A bill? On a Friday night?"

I sighed and finished filling the salt and pepper shakers on the tables. "You don't want to know."

"Is everything okay?"

"Yeah, of course. Things are fine." I looked out at the water and barely stifled a heavy sigh.

"Uh huh." She flipped the open sign to closed and started tallying receipts. "I haven't known you for long, but I know when you're full of it. Things aren't okay. I suspect it's man troubles, but that's only because with a young woman your age it's almost always man troubles, isn't it?"

I gave her a genuine smile as I walked into the kitchen untying my apron. "I wouldn't know."

She laughed and then paused. "Wait, what?"

I leaned against the walk-in cooler. "I've never really been in a relationship. So, while I don't disagree with you that it's almost always man troubles, I don't have personal experience. Except..."

"Except?"

I forced myself to remain calm—not to allow the hurt and anger to get the better of me. "I thought there might be something with a guy. I don't know. I hoped leaving my last job would clear things up between us. It did, I guess, just not in the way I wanted. He hasn't contacted me since I left."

"Since you left—two days ago?" She laughed when I nodded. "Pumpkin, you're giving up mighty fast. He's a man. Two days isn't enough time for him to get his head out of his backside. And why haven't you gone to see him?"

"I don't know."

"Maybe *you* need to get our head out of *your* backside?" She raised her eyebrows questioningly.

I hesitated. "You think I should approach him?"

"You have to decide that for yourself. But if you want my advice, I wouldn't be sitting around waiting on a man to call. If you like him, give it a shot. If you crash and burn, at least you know. Shit or get off the pot."

Wow, exactly what my grandmother would have said, may she rest in peace. I blew out a shaky breath and shook out my hands. "I'm terrified of a crash and burn."

"Well, if it does come to that, Mr. Bryan, one of the breakfast regulars, has had his eye on you."

Mr. Bryan was a stooped, white-haired, wrinkled ninety-something who shuffled around the island with a walker. "Not funny." I waved her off and headed out.

One of the amazing things about my new job at Susie's Bayfront Diner was that it came with a small studio apartment over the diner that Susie allowed me to stay in rent free for as long as I worked for her.

Just behind the bed and breakfast, I climbed the stairs to the apartment and paused for a moment on the staircase to appreciate the sun lowering over the water. Bright pink and orange clouds dotted the sky. Susie's advice had given me a sliver of hope, like maybe things could work out with Dmitry.

Already my life was looking up. It turned out that I was pretty good at waiting tables and I was also adept at lending a hand in the kitchen. I'd always loved to cook. Susie had also encouraged me to take breaks between busy times to sit in the corner and use her laptop to work on my writing.

The only things in my life that were still problematic were Nicky and Dmitry. Nicky Knuckles was going to be around for a long time. I was making less at Susie's than I had been at P.O.L.A.R., but the tips weren't bad. I accepted that I'd be paying him off for the rest of my life. I just hoped he'd stop pressuring me for more.

Dmitry...just thinking of him made my heart ache yet I couldn't stop thinking of him. I'd had this naïve fantasy that he might come after me. He hadn't. Susie was right, though. If I ever wanted to have the conversation with him about what was going on between us, I needed to just do it. If he didn't want anything to do with me, at least I'd know.

Something in my heart held fast to the hope that it wouldn't go that way. I felt a bond with Dmitry and I wanted to believe that he felt it too and that it meant something big. I wanted to believe that we were mates.

I was being incredibly starry-eyed. Dmitry had walked away from me so many times. That was probably a strong sign that I wasn't his mate.

I'd still try. I dressed in my emerald green dress and let my hair fall and fan out around my shoulders. I took extra care with my makeup and even ditched my thick glasses for contacts—something I only did on very special occasions. I wanted to do everything in my power to make it hard for Dmitry to walk away from me.

I had to meet Nicky first, but as soon as that was over, I was going to find Dmitry and demand that we have a talk.

I was supposed to meet up with Nicky Knuckles at a place called

Cap'n Jim's Bar and Grill, but as I strolled down the beach, headed in that direction, I practically ran smack dab into Nicky. I had the payment all ready for him since I certainly didn't want to draw out our interaction any longer than absolutely necessary. As I reached into my purse to pull out the money, he reached into his pocket and pulled out a knife.

My stomach dropped and I worried that I was actually going to lose control of my bladder. I knew the threat in front of me was real. Nicky Knuckles didn't play around.

"I take it you and your boyfriend aren't in communication?"

I frowned. "What are you talking about?"

For every step I took backward, Nicky Knuckles took a step forward. "Your boyfriend paid off your debt days ago. Ten G's. I was debating how to collect the interest when, lo and behold, I got your text. Talk about a stroke of luck!"

I thrust the money at him, my brain struggling to keep up with both what he was saying and the flashing blade in front of me. Dmitry had paid off my debt? What the hell? "Please take the money. Just take it."

He grinned and moved in closer. "That measly stack of bills isn't gonna cut it. Sorry, sweetheart, but I need to make an example outta you. I can't have others thinking I've gone soft."

I had only one way out and it was a longshot. I prayed that the suspicions I had about Dmitry and I being mates were real and that, if so, that we had enough of a bond that this would work. Then, instead of screaming out loud, I closed my eyes and screamed inside, as loud and as powerfully as I could. If there was a chance that we had bonded in some way, maybe he'd sense me. Then, just to be sure, I opened my eyes, met Nicky's sinister gaze, and screamed with every ounce of lung power in my chest.

My scream was cut short when Nicky's fist connected with my face.

24

DMITRY

J sat straight up in bed and let out a violent roar—a verbal decree of the rage and fury suddenly coursing through me. I could sense Kerrigan's fear and desperation in my head as though she'd shouted it into my ear. Seconds later, I heard an actual scream. I was already running down the stairs when it ceased abruptly.

My heart ached. She had to be okay.

Alexei was right behind me. "I heard it, too. What's going on?"

I didn't take the time to answer. I sprinted out into the sand and pushed my body to get to her faster. Down the beach, I saw her on the ground, her hands covering her face.

That fucking loan shark was standing over, a flash of silver in his hand. Knife. He was holding a knife on her.

"No one's coming for you, bitch. It's just you and me."

My bear was halfway out already, my body stuck in mid-shift, a visual that was one hundred percent monster. It made me faster, made me more vicious. Bloodthirst like I'd never felt demanded his life and this time, I was going to give in to the beast.

Nicholas Palermo had no idea what was coming until it was too late. By the time he heard us and his head snapped around to see us rushing him, he was already a dead man. I slammed into his body, hard, and sent him flying away from Kerrigan. I threw myself on top of him, snarling down at him with every ounce of vengeance I had for him in that moment.

The fear in his eyes just heightened my need to kill. I bared my teeth and raised my arm, claws fully formed and out.

He screamed.

I sank my claws into his chest, cutting off his scream and ending him.

The night was filled with the sound of my panting, the fury I felt still blinding me, demanding retribution, for extorting extra money from Kerrigan, for threatening to sell her into sex slavery, for the other women he'd threatened. Who knew how many of those threats he'd actually followed through on? Kerrigan had said something about him having girls in Miami who serviced clients. Death wasn't good enough for this creep. I finally let my bear fully take over. He had none of the hesitation I had about taking a human life. He fully embraced the cycle of life and death.

The life had already drained out of the asshole, but my bear was still consumed with the desire to make it right. He ripped and tore and shredded until he started to calm down.

When we turned, the entire unit had encircled Kerrigan, guarding her. They were too close to my mate, though. I was too far gone. I snarled a menacing growl, a warning to get away from her—or else.

Serge stepped out in front, his arms raised. "She's safe, brother. She's safe. You need to calm down before you go near her, though. You could hurt her."

I roared out my anger at him. I would never hurt her. She was mine to protect. I moved closer, my growls echoing through the night. They needed to get the fuck away from her.

"Dmitry, stop!" When that didn't work, Serge balled his fists up at his side and let out a heavy exhale, preparing to shift and fight.

Kerrigan squeeze between them, and dodged their attempts to keep her away from me. In a calmer state, I would've thanked them for trying to protect her from my animal who was still showing signs of being bloodthirsty.

She held out her hands, palms up. They were trembling, but she still closed the gap between us and stared at me with tear-filled eyes. "Are you okay?"

I sniffed her hands and snorted. The scent of her was soothing to my bear who was starting to come down and see things more clearly. I rubbed my face against her and huffed out a breath. *Mate.* I pushed even farther into her space, needing more.

Her arms locked around my neck as I almost knocked her over. She choked back a sob and stroked my fur.

I could smell her tears and see the bloody smudges I was leaving on her skin and clothing. Needing to comfort her more than I was able to as a bear, I shifted back and caught her in my arms when she stumbled forward.

"Get cleaned up and take care of her. We'll take care of this, Dmitry." Serge stepped forward and nodded to me. "You did the right thing, protecting her."

Alexei nodded and stepped closer. "You saved her."

I couldn't think past making sure she was okay. I was still feeling slightly crazed, though, and I needed to get her away from them. I pulled back enough to look into her eyes. What I saw there made my heart squeeze painfully. "I'm not going to hurt you."

She nodded, but if the roundness of her eyes was any indication, she was still terrified. Then I realized I still had blood all over me and it probably didn't help relieve her fear any.

"The ocean. I'm going to walk us down to the water, okay?"

She nodded again, her hands starting to come lose from around me, but I couldn't let her go. I needed to maintain contact. I easily lifted her into my arms and carried her away from the gruesome remains. I didn't put her down until I was hip deep in the water.

"I'm sorry."

She blinked a few times and shook her head. "Sorry? You saved me. You came."

"I heard you."

"You heard me scream?"

"I heard you here." I gently tapped her temple. "I'm sorry, Kerrigan.

That should never have happened. I should've done a better job of keeping you safe."

"Are you my mate?" She phrased the question as a statement, anger coloring her tone. "That's what that means, right? We're mates."

I nodded.

"Why didn't...? Why did you stay away from me?"

I couldn't tell her what I was feeling while we were both covered in her enemy's blood. "Can we talk after?"

She held my gaze and nodded. "Okay."

I set her on her feet and ran my hands over myself, scrubbing all the blood off me. Kerrigan watched and then held her breath when I moved closer and poured handfuls of water over her skin. The blood rinsed free and left goosebumps behind.

"I don't want to go back to P.O.L.A.R." She looked off in the distance behind me. "I have my own place now. Can we talk there?"

I knew about the tiny apartment over the diner. I nodded and as we left the water, I found that not only had the team made quick work of disposing of the body as though it had never been there, but someone had also left a towel and pair of shorts for me.

As I let Kerrigan lead the way, my heart pounded painfully in my chest. She was too quiet. I was terrified of what she was thinking. I knew she was mad and she'd been scared, but I had passed the point of no return. I could no longer live without her.

KERRIGAN

J had thoughts banging around in my head like ping pong balls as I led Dmitry back to my efficiency apartment. The walk up the stairs and into the small space that made up the kitchen, living room and bedroom, held tension in in every step. I motioned for him to follow me into the bathroom where I turned on the shower.

Testing the water temperature, I hesitated before stepping back. I knew Dmitry was right behind me, watching and waiting. I didn't know quite what to say, though. He'd saved my life. He'd shown up and fought for me—been my hero.

"You should clean up better." I forced my legs to move backward, and stepped out of the shower. I edged around Dmitry and motioned for him to get in as I turned my back to him. "I'll get you a clean towel."

There was still blood on the towel he'd been carrying as well as on him. There had been blood everywhere. Even down the back of his head and neck. His broad shoulders were still streaked in it. He'd killed. For me! I'd seen the truth in his eyes in those moments afterwards. He'd do it again. And again. He would've attacked his friends if they'd been any closer to me. The animal in him had been unleashed and I finally got a good look at it. I supposed it had always been there, at the back of his eyes, something hungry and dangerous.

I wasn't afraid of his bear, though, even if I should've been. He'd ripped Nicky to shreds with eight inch claws that were sharper than any knife I'd ever seen. He'd snarled and growled, wildly, viciously, ferociously. Yet...I wasn't afraid of him.

Dmitry was darker and more dangerous than I'd realized, but that shouldn't have surprised me. The things the team did, their job, it wasn't easy. He'd probably had to use deadly force more than a few times. Yet, I knew instinctually that he'd never hurt me. Just as I knew my own reflection in the mirror, I knew it. I wasn't afraid of him.

I heard him step into the shower, heard the water hitting his body. My temperature climbed higher. There was so much that needed to be said. We had to talk and I needed to know why he'd been avoiding me when it was clear that we were mates. But, before any of that, I needed to touch him and feel him next to me.

I didn't give myself time to stress about it. I didn't stop to worry about how it might or might not be perceived. I stopped being scared for once in my life.

Shit or get off the pot.

I turned to face the shower and found him watching me, the water hitting the back of his shoulders and running down his back. My heart skipped a beat, a little stumble, but it didn't change my mind. I swallowed and took the first step towards him.

Sliding my dress of one shoulder and then the other, I took another step closer. The steam from the shower filled the bathroom and fogged the mirror, and I was so glad I'd decided to wear contacts. My already wet dress clung to me, and I peeled it off of my chest and pushed it over my hips to drop at my feet.

Completely naked, I moved closer.

Dmitry's breath caught in his throat. I could sense his desire.

My chest rose and fell faster, my hand shook. My mind was steady, though. I needed him right then.

Dmitry stayed still, his eyes smoldering. They locked with mine until I was right in front of him. Drops of water splashed over his shoulders and onto me. His eyes followed the droplets. Still, he didn't touch me. His erection jutted out between us, proving his arousal, but he kept his hands at his sides. They balled into tightly clenched fists when I reached behind him for the soap and my stomach just barely grazed his erection.

I lathered my hands and focused on the sound of his breathing. Ragged and strained, I could feel how much control he was exerting. I could feel his need to touch me. Yet, he let me take control.

What I wanted was to touch and explore every part of him. I didn't feel like an unsophisticated virgin. I felt like a passionate, sensual woman who was wild about the man in front of her. I wanted to learn every single inch of his body and what he liked and didn't like. Right then, I'd start by running my soapy hands over him and, who knew, maybe then I'd run a little more over them.

I held his gaze as I placed my hands on his chest. I could see that darker part of him there, too, in the depths of his eyes, watching me almost like I was prey. Now that I'd met the darkness, seen it first hand, I knew that it was his bear I was witnessing. He may look at me as though I'm prey, but I was who and what he'd protect with his life and fight to the death for.

I washed Dmitry's chest and his stomach, my soapy hand dipping low enough to have his stomach tensing and his breath hiking. Still, I didn't go where he needed. I lathered my hands again and stepped in closer, trapping his shaft between us while I ran my hands over his sides and then up his arms. Skirting around behind him, I sighed at the sight of his back. Beautiful and so strong, I took extra care washing it. Stretching to reach his shoulders and neck, I then washed down and over his ass.

Dmitry's fists clenched and unclenched and I knew he was struggling to let me continue rather than taking the lead, but he let me clean him. I squatted behind him to clean the back of his legs and moved around to run my hands up the front of his knees and thighs. Looking up at him, I saw the glow of his animal in his gaze, but still, he held strong. I let the tip of his cock drag over my body as I slowly stood, and then reached up to cup his chin. Pulling lightly, I ran my hands over his face, taking care to trail my fingertips over his lips.

My body pulsed, every part of me readying itself for him. I shook with desire, but I wasn't finished. I rinsed his face before lathering my hands again and stepped in closer.

Holding his gaze, I cupped his erection and bit my lip as a low growl escaped the back of his throat, but he still remained perfectly still. His pupils dilated as I stroked his length, rubbing both of my hands back and forth, slowly up and down every inch of him. I dropped one hand lower to clean him there, too.

Instead of feeling self-conscious about never having done it before, I felt powerful because of his reaction. The man and animal both watched me, radiating lust and hunger, but still, I was in command of both of them.

I stroked him until all pretense of cleaning him was gone. I watched his face change, his jaw clench harder. I wanted him to come apart in my hands, wanted to see him tumble over the precipice of that control he was clinging to.

When it happened and I felt his seed splash against my stomach, I only wanted more. I knelt in front of him and slid him into my mouth, finishing him that way.

Dmitry's hands locked in my hair and before I'd finished stroking him with my tongue, he pulled me up to my feet and backed me against the cold shower wall behind me. His eyes blazed and I found myself surrendering—to anything he wanted to do to me. Anything.

26

DMITRY

I'd held back for as long as I could, letting Kerrigan slowly torture me. I'd stayed still while she took control, did what she wanted, and I enjoyed every second of her delicious exploration. But I couldn't hold back any longer. She'd been teasing more than just me. She'd been teasing the bear who'd been itching to mark and claim her. The sultry little looks that she kept casting had nearly brought me to my knees. After orgasming, I was still rock hard and ready for more of her—all of her.

I spun her under the water and made quick work of rinsing us both off before scooping her into my arms. I stepped out of the shower and carried her to the bed which was in the corner of the one-room apartment, leaving a trail of dripping water to her bed.

Her breathing was as labored as mine and her arousal perfumed the room and drove me insane, like the most exquisite torture. I tossed her onto the bed, getting an excited squeal from her.

I wanted to seduce her slowly, take my time, show her just how much I adored every part of her, but I couldn't wait. I needed to be in her, needed to make her mine, and be hers in every way. I knelt on the bed and kissed her ankle before moving up. I kissed her hip and then the valley between her breasts before capturing to her mouth. Tasting her mouth, I rested my weight on one forearm while reaching between us and running my fingers through her wet folds. She was ready for me.

I rolled my fingertip over her clit before moving lower and sliding one finger into her. Her hips tried to buck, but I was on her, keeping her steady. She bit my lip in her eagerness and I slid a second finger in, stretching her for me. Her nails dug in and scratched my back, a welcome sting. I pumped my fingers relishing in the way her body clung to them tightly. As I slid in a third finger, she broke our kiss to beg for more.

I could've listened to her sweet, breathy pleas for hours, for the rest of my life even, but I needed to be in her. I slid my fingers out and lined our bodies up. I held her gaze and released a low growl. She was mine. She was always going to be mine. No one else was ever going to threaten her or harm her again.

Her arousal had called more of my bear forward and I fought for control as I sank into her wet heat inch by inch. Her body gripped and squeezed me, pulsing around my length. More sweet torture.

Kerrigan dug into my back and her head pushed into the mattress under her while I entered her. Her exposed throat was an invitation I couldn't refuse and as I thrust the rest of my length into her, I sank my teeth into her delicate flesh, marking her as mine.

She screamed, her body clamping down on my shaft as an orgasm rocked through her. I continued to pump through it, thrusting in and out of her as the claiming mark bound us together for the rest of our lives. The bear was more in control than he should've been, but I was there, too, losing myself in her.

She lifted her legs and gripped my hips with her thighs, her hands rising from my back to my head. Holding tightly to me, she cried out my name and begged me to never stop.

I licked her neck clean to seal the ragged wound and kissed up her throat and chin. Claiming her lips again, I poured every ounce of emotion into the kiss and prayed she'd understand.

Trailing my hands down to her ass to grip her silky flesh, pulling her against me to be even deeper in her, I thrust slow and hard. The burning need to empty myself into her was growing stronger. I wanted to mark her with my seed as well—mark her in every way possible.

Kerrigan arched her back as another orgasm bloomed in her. The new angle had the tip of my shaft hitting her deeper, making her cry out louder. Her walls tightened around me until I couldn't hold back.

I pressed my forehead to hers and looked at her. "Open your eyes, mate."

Those deep brown, beautiful eyes met mine and I felt my world come together in completeness. She sank her teeth into that full lower lip and moaned. "Dmitry, please."

Another stroke and my release burst forth. Kerrigan was right there with me, milking me as we both came together. Her eyes fluttered shut and I lowered my face to her neck once more.

Everything heightened until we both collapsed together on the bed. I eased my weight off of her and held her in my arms. Holding her against me, I marveled at how everything in me—all of me—felt like it'd been taken out and shaken up. The woman pressed against my side had just turned my entire world upside down.

I drifted in and out of consciousness, still holding her. I hadn't been sleeping well since she'd left the P.O.L.A.R. house and I'd felt the need to trek to her apartment and patrol the perimeter of the place several times a night.

Having her tucked in next to me gave me allowed me to relax for the first time since I met her. Until I woke up in the middle of the night and she wasn't there.

I groggily got to my feet. I knew she was safe and nearby; I could sense her. I needed to be near her, though. My bear was still in a heightened state after feeling as though he'd almost lost her.

She was just outside the door, sitting on the landing at the top of the stairs, a blanket wrapped around her still unclothed body. She looked over her shoulder when I stepped out and raised her eyebrows at me when she noticed my shaft rising.

I ignored it and sat next to her. "What are you doing out here?"

She looked out at the ocean and smiled. It was a sad smile that tightened my stomach. "Thinking."

"About?"

"You. Me." She met my eyes and her smile faded. "Why didn't you want me? You knew we were mates..."

My chest tightened and I shook my head. I reached out for her hand, needing the physical connection. "Kerrigan, I wanted you."

Her bottom lip jutted out. "But, you didn't."

"I did from the second I saw you. It's not so simple, though..." I dragged my hand down my face and sighed. "What you saw earlier... that monster is who I am. I know I scared you, but that's not just what I do, it's who I am. I am a monster—a killer. You...you're so pure and untainted. I'm not."

She turned to stare back out at the ocean and took a deep breath. "You want to know what I thought when I saw you and Nicky Knuckles fighting?"

I frowned. "What?"

She looked back at me, her eyes intense. "I saw his knife and I thought that if he hurt you, I would find a way to kill him."

I didn't know what to say to that.

"I don't think things are as simple as good and bad, Dmitry. They can't be. What you do isn't bad. You save people." She stroked her finger down my cheek. "I'm pretty much a loser. Until Wednesday, I had a job my mom got me, no home to speak of, nothing of my own. Still a virgin, unable to hold eye contact with most people, I was ashamed of myself. Good and bad are too finite to describe people. We're all so much more complicated than a single label."

I slid my arm around her shoulder. "You're not a loser."

"And you're not a monster."

I swallowed a lump of emotion. "I don't deserve you."

"And I don't deserve you." She narrowed her eyes. "So, should we just run away from each other and act like this never happened?"

"No!" I hesitated. "Was that a jab?"

"Yeah, it was. Cause if you're going to leave and pretend like we're nothing to each other again, I need to know now."

"I'm sorry, Kerrigan. I'm sorry I made you feel like that's even a remote possibility." I sighed and gently kissed her temple. "I'm not going anywhere. You're my mate. You're stuck with me for life."

She scooted over and slid onto my lap. "Good, because your bear won't let you leave, anyway. He loooves me."

I made a confused face. "What do you mean? I mean, yes, he does, but how do you know?"

She suddenly grinned. "You talk in your sleep. Didn't you know that?"

"What? No."

"Or maybe your bear talks in your sleep. Either way, he *really* likes me."

I snorted a laugh. I felt the same way.

She laughed, the sound so beautiful and sweet, I gave her a squeeze. "And you, Dmitry?"

I stilled and looked down at her suddenly realizing what she was getting at. "You were worried I didn't feel the same way? Is that why you were out here?"

She nodded. "I was worried that you might disagree with him."

"I don't."

"Good."

"Kerrigan?"

"Yeah?"

"We're the same being, my bear and me. What he says and feels about you? It's from me, too."

She rested her cheek against my chest. "You don't even know what he said."

"Kerrigan?"

She giggled. "Yeah?"

"I love you."

She turned and flashed me the happiest smile before kissing me deeply and passionately. When she finally broke off the kiss, we were both breathing hard. "Show me."

With her wearing my fresh claiming mark, I was able to take my time this time and really show her just how much I loved her. Lost in pleasuring her, I almost missed when she whispered the words into her palm while coming apart under me.

"I love you, too."

THE END

Vilified by strangers,
    Friendships aren't Heidi's forte.
    Unless it happens to be with a displaced polar bear.
    Hey, he's a great listener!

Alexei knows she's his mate.
    But she refuses to date him.
    All he wants is a chance.

As far as he can tell, there's only one way to get near her—as a Covert Bear.
    Get Covert Bear HERE

BEARS OF BURDEN

In the southwestern town of Burden, Texas, good ol' bears Hawthorne, Wyatt, Hutch, Sterling, and Sam, and Matt are livin' easy. Beer flows freely, and pretty women are abundant. The last thing the shifters of Burden are thinking about is finding a mate or settling down. But, fate has its own plan...

1. Thorn
2. Wyatt
3. Hutch
4. Sterling
5. Sam
6. Matt

* * *

SHIFTERS OF HELL'S CORNER

In the late 1800's, on a homestead in New Mexico, a female shifter named Helen Cartwright, widowed under mysterious circumstances, knew there was power in the feminine bonds of sisterhood. She provided an oasis for those like herself, women who had been dealt the short end of the stick. Like magic, women have flocked to the tiny town of Helen's Corner ever since. Although, nowadays, some call the town by another name, **Hell's Crazy Corner.**

1. Wolf Boss
2. Wolf Detective
3. Wolf Soldier
4. Bear Outlaw
5. Wolf Purebred

* * *

DRAGONS OF THE BAYOU

Something's lurking in the swamplands of the Deep South. Massive creatures exiled from their home. For each, his only salvation is to find his one true mate.

1. Fire Breathing Beast
2. Fire Breathing Cezar
3. Fire Breathing Blaise
4. Fire Breathing Remy
5. Fire Breathing Armand
6. Fire Breathing Ovide

* * *

RANCHER BEARS

When the patriarch of the Long family dies, he leaves a will that has each of his five son's scrambling to find a mate. Underneath it all, they find that family is what matters most.

1. Rancher Bear's Baby
2. Rancher Bear's Mail Order Mate
3. Rancher Bear's Surprise Package
4. Rancher Bear's Secret
5. Rancher Bear's Desire
6. Rancher Bears' Merry Christmas

Rancher Bears Complete Box Set

* * *

KODIAK ISLAND SHIFTERS

On Port Ursa in Kodiak Island Alaska, the Sterling brothers are kind of a big deal.
They own a nationwide chain of outfitter retail stores that they grew from their father's little backwoods camping supply shop.
The only thing missing from the hot bear shifters' lives are mates! But, not for long...

1. Billionaire Bear's Bride (COLTON)
2. The Bear's Flamingo Bride (WYATT)
3. Military Bear's Mate (TUCKER)

* * *

SHIFTERS OF DENVER

Nathan: Billionaire Bear- A matchmaker meets her match.
Byron: Heartbreaker Bear- A sexy heartbreaker with eyes for just one woman.
Xavier: Bad Bear - She's a good girl. He's a bad bear.

1. Nathan: Billionaire Bear
2. Byron: Heartbreaker Bear
3. Xavier: Bad Bear

Shifters of Denver Complete Box Set

Made in the USA
Coppell, TX
28 March 2022

75671682R00080